Love Is Like Water

Arab American Writing

Selected titles from Arab American Writing

In memory of my father

SAMIA SERAGELDIN is the author of an autobiographical novel, *The Cairo House* (Syracuse University Press, 2000), and a historical novel, *The Naqib's Daughter* (2009), as well as short stories and political essays, most recently in *Women Writing Africa* (2009), *Muslim Networks from Haj to Hip-Hop* (2005), and *In the Name of Osama bin Laden* (2002).

Contents

Acknowledgment

Heartfelt thanks are due to my editor, Mary Selden Evans.

Love Is Like Water

Reading Jane Austen in Cairo

In my great-grandmother's generation, women were sometimes taught to read but not to write, specifically to forestall
the possibility that they might be swindled out of their fortune—or their honor, if they were to write love letters. My
grandmother, *Sitt* Luli, had learned to read and write, of
course, but she had never learned how to handle money, a failing that would eventually have the gravest consequences.

"Sitt Luli" was the affectionate nickname by which my
paternal grandmother was called in her family, very much
along the lines of the "Miss Elly" or "Miss Libby" that you
still hear in the American South. I never heard either of my
grandmothers addressed by her first name. For that generation, a woman's first name was not bandied about lightly; the
household help referred to them as "the Elder Sitt" to distin-
guish them from their daughters. They kept their maiden
names after marriage, like all Muslim women, but for public
matters like newspaper announcements of marriages and
obituaries, they went from being referred to as *karimat* so-
and-so, a euphemism for daughter, to *haram* so-and-so, wife.
In our social circle, at least, they were spared the ultimate
designation-by-male-relative: the ubiquitous *Om* so-and-so
or mother of so-and-so.

Sitt Luli was a small woman, and you would never have
guessed from her unassuming air that she had brought the

bulk of the land into the family. I knew this, even as a child, and when I was slightly older and read Jane Austen, it never failed to astonish me that Austen's English heroines and their families were invariably threatened with dispossession and destitution for the lack of a male heir. I took it for granted that both my grandmothers, and my mother, had inherited from their fathers.

But heiress that she was, Sitt Luli was embarrassingly unworldly and gullible: inexpensive trifles pleased her more than fine jewelry, and she was rumored to occasionally buy shoes at a children's store rather than order them at her shoemaker's. She could not be bothered with paperwork, and would sign whatever was given to her without scrutiny. One of her sons, the proverbial black sheep, took advantage of this habit, periodically inducing her to sign over to him small pieces of property. Her other children remonstrated gently with her, but there was nothing to be done.

For that matter, as soon as she could, she had turned over the running of the household to her oldest daughter, Nazmia, as tall and commanding as my grandmother was small and unassertive. My aunt Nazmia ran the house with an iron hand during her tenure, disciplining her younger brothers by making them stand in a corner with a heavy bunch of keys hanging around their ears like a bunch of grapes on the vine. The uncle who grew up to be the black sheep always claimed that his ears stuck out from his head as a result of frequent such disciplining.

The photo portrait that I have of Sitt Luli must have been taken when she was about forty. In the photo, her dark hair is expertly waved; she is made up in the Hollywood fashion of the thirties, with pencil-thin arched brows and bow lips; her manicured hands with dark nail polish are folded in front of her. In spite of the makeup there is something ill-defined about her features. She is looking away from the camera, expressionless. She looks as if she had been made up and coiffed just for the occasion, and as if this portrait was not her idea.

I remember my father carrying her like a child up and down the stairs of our villa the year she died. That winter, whenever there was a particularly cold spell, Sitt Luli showed up at our door in her outdated black Bentley, driven by her old Sudanese driver, with her equally ancient maid sitting in the front seat beside him. Grandmother had come to take a bath. She caught chills bathing in her own big, drafty bathroom in the family house with its cathedral ceilings. The first time she had visited my parents' new villa in Zamalek, she had been impressed by nothing as much as the modern bathrooms.

"Oh, how cozy they are!" she'd exclaimed. "Why, one would never catch cold bathing in these bathrooms!"

In Grandmother's bathroom in the family house, there were three tall, creaky, wooden double doors, one leading to the bedroom, one to the adjoining boudoir—now the maid's room—and one to the corridor outside. The monstrous bathtub was screened off by a curtain; only its big brass clawed feet were visible, and the stool that was used to climb into it. A table held loofahs, white and black pumice stones, and towels. At one end, a screen provided privacy for the WC with its wooden tank suspended overhead, and for the bidet with its stack of washcloths. At the other end stood a vanity with a huge gilded-frame mirror, a chair, and a wooden wardrobe. A palpable draft nipped my ankles whenever I stood between the door to the corridor and the door to the maid's room.

Papa and Mama had immediately insisted that Sitt Luli must come to our house to take her baths. At first she wouldn't hear of it, but having caught a chill twice already that winter, she was finally prevailed upon. Her final objection was that she could not climb the stairs in the new villa; in the family house there was a rickety oak and wrought-iron elevator installed to ride between the ground floor and the second. So when she came to our house Papa made sure to be on hand to pick her up and carry her up the stairs with as much ease as if she had been a child. After her bath she retired immediately to bed, where hot water bottles would have been placed, and stayed there till the next morning, when she would go home.

Sitt Luli had other eccentricities; her phobia about germs was a social liability. She draped a sheer scarf over her hand whenever she needed to shake hands with people, under the pretext that she had washed for prayer. I was too young to see through that flimsy excuse; touching the hand of an adult male who was not a close relative might require a woman to go through her ablutions again before prayer, but my grandmother did this even when shaking hands with other women. Only close family members were exempt.

My favorite of the stories that circulated in the family about her naïveté had to do with the air raids over Cairo during the Suez War. Whenever the air raid sirens went off, everyone in the house had instructions to take cover in the cellars. "Everyone" included the twenty-odd family members: the grandmother; her eldest son the Pasha, and his wife and children; the next two eldest sons and their families; unmarried younger sons; plus the thirty-odd servants.

The family had moved to the new European neighborhood, Garden City, shortly after the First World War, when their old neighborhood across the Nile, Manial, was becoming unfashionable.

But the first time the sirens sounded, Sitt Luli was nowhere to be found. The family and servants followed instructions and scrambled down to the kitchen cellars, while the Pasha directed the evacuation from a chair in the middle of the vast hall. Like the captain of a sinking ship, he waited to go down to the shelter himself until every last soul in the house had been accounted for. But the Elder Sitt was missing. The blackout was in force, and they searched for her high and low, candles in hand. They looked for her behind the high-backed velvet sofas of the outer salon and the gilt needlepoint chairs of the inner salon; behind the bookcases in the gloomy, wood-paneled study with its stained glass window; in the darkest recesses of the twenty-four-chair dining room; in each of the several bedroom suites upstairs; in the bathrooms and the boudoirs and the children's rooms; in the "lost" rooms under the marble staircase; even in the rickety wrought-iron elevator.

The grandmother was nowhere to be found. In desperation, they were about to start searching the maids' rooms on the top floor; the menservants' quarters were in a separate building. Then someone thought to look in the large armoire in her own bedroom and found her huddled there. They brought her downstairs to the Pasha, who persuaded her that it was much safer to go down to the cellar.

"But you must come too," she objected.

"Don't worry about me, Mama dear," he reassured her, quite disingenuously. "The chair I'm sitting on is the safest spot in the house."

"In that case, dear," she replied, not missing a beat, "get up and give me your seat."

It was around that time that matters came to a head with the black sheep. The family discovered that Sitt Luli had deeded to him a large property that he had promptly sold in order to finance one of his ventures, forcing them to buy back the property for nearly triple the price in order to keep the headwaters of the estate intact.

This time a serious conclave of the siblings was convened and it was decided that something must be done. Sitt Luli was persuaded to deed her entire property and assets to her children, each according to his share of her inheritance. She signed off with no more reluctance than she would a shoemaker's bill. In effect, for her, nothing much had changed; she had never handled her own finances in the first place, and she continued to sign off as usual on whatever bills she incurred.

As her younger sons and daughters married and gradually moved to villas or apartments of their own in Cairo, Sitt Luli adopted a regular schedule according to which she did the rounds of her children's homes, having dinner with a different son or daughter every day. Since she had more children than days of the week, she never had dinner at home in the family house, much to the displeasure of her eldest son. "But Mama," he remonstrated, "all I am asking you to do is to set aside a day to have dinner with me at home, as you do with the others." The Pasha was a very busy man, with many responsibilities in the cabinet and the party, so dinner—the main meal, served in the early afternoon—was the only time he had to spend with family.

But Sitt Luli continued to make her rounds, and with her usual vagueness often seemed to confuse the days of the week. My father, the youngest, was her favorite, and sometimes she showed up at our villa when it was not her appointed day to do so, in her weathered black car, driven by her old chauffeur and accompanied by her maid. My mother always greeted her with genuine enthusiasm, and she would call my father home from wherever he was. In those days, before the expropriation and nationalization decrees, my parents kept what was called an open house; drop-in guests were more than welcome. The problem was the justifiable indignation of the aunt or uncle whose turn had been passed over. Whenever my grandmother was expected at someone else's house and was more than a few minutes late, her known weakness for my father made him the usual suspect, and we would receive irate phone calls from one aunt or another demanding to know if Sitt Luli was at our house.

I remember that, when I was seven, I was coached to offer her my condolences on her brother's death. "May the rest of his life prolong yours," I rehearsed, over and over, in the car as we drove toward Garden City. I was specifically cautioned not to confuse that phrase with another formulaic phrase proffered on happy occasions like engagements and weddings: "May your turn be next." The two phrases sound very similar in Arabic. Sure enough, when I stood before my grandmother and the dozens of ladies assembled in the salon to pay their condolences, I blurted out, "May your turn be next." There was a moment of consternation—Egyptians are great believers in ill omens—and then Sitt Luli laughed.

All the same, though, she was dead within the year.

Dying just when she did, she was spared the worst of what was to follow for her family. But when she passed away, even President Nasser sent an official representative to walk in her funeral cortege and sign the book of condolences.

Her obituary listed her as the dearly departed of the such-and-such families; "karimat so-and-so . . . , haram of . . . , and mother of . . . ," followed by a three-column list of relatives, as was proper and fitting. And there it was, her real name, plain and unqualified, at last: Zakia—"the intelligent one."

The Modernizing Project of the Egyptian Family

Even in carefully compartmentalized lives, there are moments when the past ambushes you in the most unlikely time and place imaginable. I was moderating a panel at the annual conference of the Middle East Studies Association in Washington, D.C., when one of the presenters leaned across the table and passed me a blurred photocopy from a microfiche: a page from an Egyptian society magazine dated over a half-century ago. Her presentation was titled "The Modernizing Project of the Egyptian Family in the Mid-twentieth Century as Reflected in Print Media." She had prepared slides of cartoons and articles from Egyptian periodicals of that era that she planned to use to illustrate her talk. In the course of her research, she whispered to me with one hand over the microphone as she handed me the paper, she had come across this particular article and, recognizing the family connection, thought it would interest me.

I nodded and thanked her and introduced the first speaker; the researcher who had handed me the paper was slated last. I sneaked discreet glances at the copy in my hand. The article featured a monthly column called "His Story/Her Story," in which a fashionable Cairo couple were interviewed and asked how they met and married. The two accounts were juxtaposed, accompanied by photographs. The couple in question were my uncle Zakariah, three years older than my father, and his bride, Nimette, a beauty from a distinguished Turkish family. The interview was taken on the eve of the revolution of 1952.

In her photo, she wears a charming little hat over her honey-brown curls, and her dimpled smile is dazzling; he is wearing a neat moustache and an elegant, almost dandy-ish suit. The husband lists among the accomplishments that attracted him to his future bride her fluency in French, Italian, English and Turkish, in addition to Arabic. He describes her as "the girl of my dreams," and she returns the compliment, adding that he is her "best friend." They share similar tastes in music, and they both love dancing and nightlife.

I could see how the article illustrated perfectly the modern self-image of a certain class of young Egyptian couples of the early fifties. I wondered, a little apprehensively, if the researcher intended to use the article about my uncle in the course of her presentation. I sneaked another glance at the page in my lap.

In his account of meeting his future wife, Zakariah relates how his oldest brother, the Pasha, had brought a photograph in a society magazine to his attention, asking, "What do you think of this beautiful girl?"

"Very lovely, indeed."

"No, I mean what do you think of her as a prospective bride? Such a pretty girl would be an asset to the family, and her background is excellent. Shall I arrange a casual meeting at the Gezira Club?"

I recognized my eldest uncle in that account; he had an eye for pretty things—women, jewelry, antiques—and his impulse was to acquire them for the family. It was like him, too, to decide when it was time for one of his playboy younger brothers to settle down, and to act without delay once he had decided.

The Pasha himself, and the two next older brothers, had done their duty to the family dynasty by marrying cousins with large estates adjoining their own; they were wed to pleasant, familiar, not particularly glamorous women a year or two older than themselves. The three younger brothers had been free to choose their own brides. One, the proverbial black sheep, married early and often; he was to accumulate four marriages and three divorces over the years. The youngest, Murad, my father, had just become engaged to an attractive young heiress of unimpeachable upbringing.

That left the second youngest brother, Zakariah, still unmarried in his mid-twenties. Zakariah was over six feet tall and large, with apricot freckles and reddish hair he damped down to auburn with pomade. In response to one of the questions in the "His Story/Her Story" article, Nimette praises his sweetness and generosity, but complains of his pride and temper, whereas he praises her pliability and obedience and denies that she has any faults at all. As it turns out, she was perceptive, while he was oblivious, or perhaps merely gallant.

In fact their courtship was fraught with pitfalls. Zakariah came from a large, boisterous clan used to living their lives with very little privacy. The sprawling Garden City house teemed with brothers and sisters-in-law and children and servants; relatives and friends came and went without notice at all times of the day and late into the night; party officials and retainers hung about the study waiting for the

Pasha to return from cabinet meetings. The kitchen and pantries were constantly churning to serve meals to twenty extra people at the drop of a hat and the *suffragis* shuttled back and forth with refreshments as successive waves of guests arrived and departed.

Nimette, on the other hand, was the younger of two daughters of a distinguished Turkish father, raised by her Swiss stepmother in a home as refined and quiet and carefully calibrated as a Swiss watch. The first time Zakariah came for a prolonged visit to his prospective fiancée, he lost track of the time until she looked at her watch and asked him if he were staying to lunch; she would need to let the cook know. The mere idea of asking, rather than assuming, indeed insisting, that a guest stay when mealtimes came around shocked Zakariah; as for the notion that a cook needed to be given advance notice of a single extra guest, he found that unfathomable. He took his leave in something of a huff.

But he came back the next day, duly invited this time, and sat down with her father, stepmother, and sister in the elegant dining room of their airy, sunny villa overlooking the Nile in the most sought-after neighborhood in Zamalek. He was impressed by the meticulous service but taken aback by the simplicity of the perfectly executed menu: cream of celery soup, grilled steak, salad, and crème brulée.

An hour or so later, in the bustling dining room of the Garden City house, over a second lunch of rabbit with green soup, roast shoulder of lamb with vermicelli, and pigeons stuffed with cracked wheat, Zakariah shared his disconcerting experience with the family.

The Pasha mulled this over for a minute. "It must be the Swiss influence," he finally remarked.

"The whole family must be on a diet," his sister Nazmia speculated. "Now we know how Nimette stays so slim."

"The soup was actually hot," Zakariah marveled, "served in individual covered bowls." In the Garden City house, a constant complaint was that the food was never served warm enough; by the time dishes made their way up in the dumbwaiters and were handed from one suffragi to another, they had inevitably cooled.

"Well, in a house this size," the Pasha's wife, Doria, shrugged defensively, "you can't expect otherwise."

"But seriously," Zakariah shook his head, "if we get married and have our own home, what if I can't bring half a dozen friends over for lunch without advance notice? Can you imagine how embarrassing that would be?"

"When you are married and have your own home, I am sure your young bride will quickly learn our ways and keep an open house you can be proud of," the Pasha reassured him.

The three older brothers lived with their families in the Garden City house; the sisters had moved to their husbands' homes when they married years ago; the three younger brothers, it was understood, would set up their own homes, buying apartments or building villas.

"The book was written" between Murad and his fiancée, Faiza; that is, the signing of their marriage contract had already taken place, so legally they were man and wife, and therefore free to go out together without a chaperone. Zakariah and Nimette were only engaged, but her father was less conservative and allowed them to court with relative freedom.

The two young women spent considerable time that spring shopping for their trousseaus together. They attended fashion shows of the "New Look" launched by exciting young French couturiers like Dior, Balmain, and Balenciaga. The two young women's tastes were as different as their styles: Faiza set off her taller, hourglass shape and long black hair with dramatic shades of red; Nimette enhanced her petite, fair looks with pastel tones and softer styles. Murad found fashion deadly boring, and was happy to leave it to his brother to accompany the two girls to *défilés* and trunk shows. Zakariah did not mind in the least; he took an active interest in Nimette's appearance.

"Wasn't she wearing that same white piqué dress Thursday at the sports club?" he complained in an undertone to his future sister-in-law Faiza, as Nimette disappeared into a fitting room.

"Come to think of it, she was, but I hadn't noticed, she's so clever with accessorizing. She was wearing it with a pink scarf and pink sandals Thursday, and today she's dressed it up with a black belt and pumps and pearls. She always looks perfect, though, I only wish I could look so good in everything."

Nimette came out of the fitting room in a cocktail gown with a bustier-style bodice and a very full, stiff skirt of black tulle over peach satin.

"It's stunning!" Faiza applauded.

"What do you think, Zakariah?" Nimette twirled before him.

He frowned. "It's rather bare, isn't it?"

"We can whip up a tulle wrap to drape over the shoulders and back," suggested the couturier's assistant. "Just a wisp of tulle but it would give a suggestion of coverage."

"In that case it will be all right."

"We might need to take the skirt up an inch as well. Perhaps you can come back for a fitting tomorrow when Monsieur Bertrand himself can take a look." The assistant escorted Nimette back to the fitting room.

"Faiza, I want your advice about something before Nimette comes back." Zakariah spoke in a hurried undertone. "You know how she always wants me to go along when she's shopping for her trousseau? She always asks for my opinion about every single outfit, down to the last hat. I'm wondering if I'm not expected to pay for all this. Do you think I should offer?"

"Of course not! I would be very offended in her place. I wouldn't dream of letting Murad pay for a single stitch of my trousseau."

In defense of my mother, her father's death had made her an heiress at the age of thirteen, and she had never known what it was like not to have an independent income. It had also occurred to her that Zakariah might have been asking on behalf of his brother as well as himself, and that consideration contributed to the categorical tone of her response.

The next day an uncharacteristically somber Zakariah asked Murad and Faiza to meet him urgently at the Garden City house. While they waited in the library for the Pasha to finish his phone call and join the conversation, Zakariah announced that he had had a fight with Nimette and that they had broken off their engagement.

"First of all, I went to pick her up from a fitting after the trunk show at the atelier. The assistants asked me to wait in the salon but I heard a man's voice inside the fitting room so I was having none of that, I walked right in. I found her in her bustier and petticoat with this French *khawaga* pinning up her skirt. You can imagine the scene I made! And she accused me of acting *baladi!* Me!" Zakaria prided himself on being the most modern and open-minded of his family— *évolué,* evolved, as the French expression went—so the accusation of acting "country" stung.

"Calm down," Murad counseled. "As for Monsieur Bertrand—these French dressmaker fellows don't really count, if you see what I mean."

"You may be right about that, but that wasn't the only thing."

The Pasha had hung up the receiver and lit his cigar, nodding for Zakariah to continue.

"Nimette then got all upset with me and called me insensitive and said I had put her in a very embarrassing position, after she'd ordered all those dresses, and I finally figured out that she had expected me to pay for her trousseau. You were wrong about that, Faiza, this mess is partly your fault!"

"Oh no! I had no idea. Poor Nimette!"

"I don't understand this," Zakariah went on. "Her father is very well off, isn't he?"

The Pasha took a long puff of his cigar. "Listen, Zakariah, she has a stepmother, so that would naturally be an influence on the father. And a Swiss stepmother at that; they must have a very different notion of how things are done, in Switzerland. But take the Syrians even, closer to home; the bridegroom pays for everything, down to the last handkerchief. If I were you, if you want Nimette, pay for everything with good grace, and keep it entirely to yourself so as to save her face in this family. She's a beautiful and accomplished girl, and you can more than afford to spoil her as she deserves to be spoilt. In your place, I would go make up with her right now."

That summer, the singer Om Kalthoum, already a legend in Egypt and the Arab world and an habitué of the Cairo House since the humble beginnings of her career, was called upon to sing twice at family weddings: first at Murad's and then at Zakariah's two months later. Nimette made a lovely bride in her Swiss-lace, pearl-encrusted wedding gown, and Zakariah beamed with pride. The courtship had not been a smooth one, by any means, but if Nimette had any misgivings about fitting in with her new husband's rather overwhelming family, it did not show in the brilliant smile of her wedding portrait.

In the optimistic years around the mid-century mark, the family into which Nimette and Faiza married was an ambitious and cohesive clan over which the Pasha rode herd with the lightest of touches. When the third of the brothers went into partnership in a new, privately held bank, the members of the family showed their support by transferring their accounts en masse to the untried new institution. The one holdout was a brother-in-law and cousin, married to Nazmia, the oldest sister. Gently pressed by the Pasha, Zulfikar Bey proposed a bargain: if the family, especially the younger brothers with their new brides, were to come to keep him company on his country estate for the three days of the Lesser Feast, he would transfer his account to the new bank.

The prospect of spending three days in utter boredom in the deepest reaches of the Delta was especially daunting to Faiza and Nimette, who, unlike the other women in the family, had not grown up accustomed to stretches of country living. The two young women accepted the bargain with good grace, but they were to pay a higher price than they expected.

On the first day of the feast, a procession of cars made the half-day's drive up from Cairo to Deir-al-Ghazal, the Zulfikar family seat in the eastern province. Their arrival at the gate was announced by a volley of celebratory gunshots fired in the air by the watchmen, and loud *zaghrutas* erupting from the *fellahas* on the rooftops. As they drove up to the house, strong aromas of spit-roasting lamb and clay-oven-baked bread wafted from the kitchens in the outbuildings. Disembarking tired and dusty, the two newlywed couples were shown to adjoining rooms in the sprawling country house. They were informed that Zulfikar Bey would be back any minute; he was overseeing the arrangements for the country wedding he had planned for the evening's entertainment. There was to be traditional stick-dueling, belly dancing, and horses trained to prance to music.

Faiza and Nimette set about unpacking, chatting through the open door connecting the two rooms, while the men went downstairs in search of refreshments. Suddenly the door to the hall burst open and there stood a man in a brown wool galabiya, the ends of his white shawl drawn over the lower half of his face, brandishing a rifle. "Where are your menfolk?" he shouted. "Do you know who I am? I am the sworn enemy of this accursed family and today I will get my revenge! Where are your menfolk?" The villager's voice cracked, and he seemed to be shaking with anger behind his shawl.

The two women clutched each other and quaked in the middle of the room; they had heard of the blood vendettas that were carried on for generations among the fellahin. As soon as they recovered the use of their voices they sensibly directed the menacing villager to look for their husbands downstairs, where they would be getting refreshments, or, as Nimette remembered helpfully, "Zakariah might well be in the billiards room if there is one in this house."

Just then Murad sauntered down the hall, a bottle of Coca Cola in hand. "Zulfikar, Zulfikar," he shook his head reproachfully, "is this any way to greet your guests?" At which the masked man dropped his shawl and leaned against the doorway, shaking so hard with laughter he could barely stand upright. It was none other than their host, Zulfikar Bey.

Nimette and Faiza never had a chance to acquire a taste for the charms of country life; the coup d'état that came to be known as the Revolution of 1952 soon put an end to the era of large cotton estates. The new regime of the colonels targeted certain politicians of the ancient regime as dangerous counterrevolutionaries: the Pasha was confined for long stretches, years at a time, to house arrest at his Garden City home. The family and close friends rallied around to entertain the patriarch. They gathered faithfully in the salons every evening, the women dressed up and bejeweled, the men in their sharkskin summer suits, cigarettes in hand. Long-running tournaments of monopoly, canasta, and bridge were organized after dinner, followed by musical entertainment and occasional private screenings of the latest films starring Omar Sharif, himself a friend of the family and a frequent hand at bridge in those days.

Looking at family photos, it strikes me that the men, and especially the women, emulated as closely as possible in dress and coiffure the Hollywood stars of that era, and that in turn Egyptian films of the period looked to their own upper classes for models of glamour. The modernizing project of the Egyptian family seemed to be well launched and inexorable.

But the photos in the family albums grew scarcer, then stopped altogether as the years wore on and the political atmosphere became increasingly repressive. The new "socialist" decrees that targeted certain families left us financially strapped and politically ostracized, and these pressures in turn began to take their toll on the personal lives of the whole clan. One uncle divorced his wife so she could keep her property under the new regulations; they remained on good terms.

Zakariah and Nimette's marriage had always been prone to flare-ups, and the arguments became more frequent and increasingly acrimonious over the years. Now that the buffers of good fortune and the easy life were stripped away, the points of friction between them rubbed increasingly raw. They were caught in a cycle of separation and reconciliation, till their families and friends were tired of interceding. The last time she walked out, Zakariah was too proud to bring her back.

The admiration of other men always lurked in the background, and Nimette remarried soon after her divorce. One day she came to see Zakariah. In the state the country was in, she pleaded, the best thing for her and for their two sons was to go to Switzerland with her new husband and make a new life there. Zakariah—himself remarried at the time to an elegant brunette from the Jordanian royal family—did what few Egyptian fathers would have considered doing: he let Nimette take his sons out of the country and out of his life.

Years later, Nimette came back from Switzerland to visit my father, Murad, on his sickbed in Cairo; he was recovering from his first serious heart attack. I was eighteen at the time and she made an indelible impression on me. Nimette must have been nearly forty, the same age as my mother, but she seemed at least a decade younger with her girlish figure and stylishly straight, long brown hair. She wore the latest look, a paisley print, bell-bottom jersey pantsuit with pointy suede boots.

Nimette perched on the edge of my father's bed and patted his hand while my uncle Zakariah stood on the other side, smiling and smoking a cigarette. They bantered with such verve and affection that, when they left, I asked my father if we should try to get them back together; they were both between marriages at the time. My father laughed at my attempt at matchmaking. "It would never work, *habibti;* it's like cat and dog with those two; sooner or later they would start fighting again."

Nimette died in Switzerland a couple of years before my uncle died in Cairo. They both outlived their health and their looks, spending their last years in sickly, self-imposed isolation of one sort or another: she living abroad, he cut off from his family by an unacceptable third marriage. It was hard to believe that the man who had once cared so much about appearances, who had taken such pride in his wife's breeding and sophistication, had contracted, late in life, a third union with a woman bereft of looks, charm, elegance, or a single redeeming grace.

Looking at the article of "His Story/Her Story" in my hand, at the photo of the pretty girl with the dimpled smile and the dapper young man with the confident look, reading their words so full of optimism and obliviousness, it seemed to me as if they belonged to an era that had come to a dead end: a dead end in evolution, like the Neanderthals, rather than a phase in the natural progression to the present moment. Today's Egypt of women in *hijab* and strict social conservatism seemed more like a direct throwback to my grandmother's generation, as if the two intervening generations, Nimette's and mine, had been an aberration, a detour in the road. I had made the mistake of thinking that evolution must have a single track.

The researcher who had so kindly made me the copy of the article stood up to take her turn at the podium before the slide projection screen in the hushed, darkened conference hall in Washington. I found myself hoping she would not use this recovered relic of my family's past to illustrate her presentation. Image after image flitted on the screen as she pointed with her laser pointer to the treasures she had unearthed from the musty archives of another place and time. Finally she wrapped up her presentation, switched off the slide projector, and motioned for someone to turn the lights back on. After the panel discussion, when we got up to leave, I thanked her again for the article. "I'm curious, though, why you didn't use it as one of your illustrations," I couldn't help asking. "Was it out of consideration for me?"

"Not really," she smiled, "it wouldn't have been appropriate anyway. I tried to use examples that would provide a model for generalizing about the rise of a modern middle class. And your family, with the political prominence, the wealth—it was hardly typical, was it?"

Love Is Like Water

"Love," my maternal grandmother, Nanou, used to say, "is like water." It took me a long time, and much grief, to understand what she meant.

Now Nanou was another proposition altogether from Sitt Luli. She was almost a whole generation younger than my father's mother, and as tall and generously built as the other was small and frail. My maternal grandmother was a force of nature, a woman to be reckoned with. In a photo of her as a little girl, she already looked determined, standing with her tummy sticking out, her hand in her father's as they posed for a formal portrait. She wore a large beribboned hat with feathers; a ruffled, low-sash dress; white stockings; and buckled shoes. Her father cut an imposing figure, with his aloof monocle and the watch chain stretching from the pocket of his frock coat across his considerable girth.

Nanou married at seventeen—a year or two late by the standards of the day—and found herself a widow at thirty-six, with six children ranging in age from eighteen to six. Her father was deceased; her only brother had married an Englishwoman and was spending his inheritance at a brisk clip in England; and she had never been close to her husband's family.

It was assumed she would remarry quickly; she had been a wealthy woman in her own right, and her husband's

23

sudden heart attack left her even more so. As the saying went, "The shadow of a man is better than the shadow of a wall." But Nanou never so much as entertained the idea of remarriage. She devoted herself to raising her six children and single-handedly ran her considerable property along with her children's inheritances from their father.

Few women of her time and place and upbringing could have managed to do what Nanou did: to deal, on her own, with overseers and fellahin; with agents and the state-appointed trustees of her husband's estate; with her daughters' suitors and her sons' peccadilloes. But manage she did, with acumen and authority. She met all the expenses of her large household out of her own pocket, refusing to touch her children's trust funds. She prided herself on handing over their intact inheritance to each of them, when they reached their majority in the case of the boys, or when they married in the case of the girls, since they married in their teens as was the custom.

By the time I knew Nanou, her greatest battles were behind her, and she had mellowed into the most loving and generous grandmother imaginable, but we were still careful to use one of her many preferred euphemisms for all kinds of expressions that offended her Victorian sensibilities. We were not allowed to refer to someone's wife as such, presumably because the word *marat* in Arabic, like *femme* in French, also meant "woman"; we were to use "his lady" instead. Once Nanou took umbrage to a word, you knew better than to ask her why; all you could do was add it to the long list of her niceties.

I remember her as a tall, heavily-built woman who nevertheless took comically tiny steps in an effort to minimize her stature. She was always exhorting my girl cousins and me to be more ladylike. When we were teenagers and clomped about in the clunky platform shoes that were the fashion for a while in the seventies, she would shake her head and tell us we sounded like night watchmen doing their rounds on country estates.

She had learned to play a few classical pieces on the piano as a child, and when we played the Beatles' "Hard Day's Night" for her she was shocked. "That's *zar*," she pronounced, referring to spirit propitiation rituals practiced in certain devotee circles in Egypt. At the time we laughed and thought Nanou didn't know what she was talking about, but of course her ears had recognized the African rhythms lurking at the heart of rock music.

After her children were grown and gone, my grandmother moved, alone, to a spacious villa in Heliopolis, a suburb of Cairo that in those days was still constructed in strict compliance with the architectural vision of Baron Empain, the Belgian entrepreneur. Every morning Nanou telephoned each of her daughters for a chat that lasted at least an hour. Every Friday, the weekend in Muslim countries, the entire family gathered around her table; anyone who was absent needed a good excuse, along the order of deathbed illness or a trip abroad. Children were kept busy cranking up batches of homemade ice cream on the verandah till everyone had arrived and the bountiful buffet in the dining room was ready.

Nanou's cook was a short, middle-aged woman literally as wide as she was tall; we nicknamed her the box because of her square, densely packed shape, topped with an incongruously small, sharp face. Her fleshy bulk apparently made her quite desirable in some circles; suitors would come to pick her up on a motorcycle on her days off. We children would rush to the balcony to watch, giggling, as she nimbly straddled the motorcycle's backseat and roared off, a wildly improbable sight.

Nanou ran her household a little like a cottage industry, distributing the overflow to her children's homes. Every so often her driver would come to our door bearing baskets of mangoes from her orchards, or jars of homemade jam, pickles, and various specialties. She had a jam-maker, a woman who came with her adult daughters by train from Nanou's farm, bearing fruits in season: the long, hard red dates in the fall; oranges for marmalade and candied peel in winter; apricots and strawberries in spring; grapes, figs and guavas in summer. In my grandmother's kitchen they cooked up huge vats of jam and ladled them into knee-high jars; some were destined for the larder and the rest to be distributed among the family's households.

Unlike my paternal grandmother, Nanou rarely visited her children's houses; she expected them to come to her. Wherever she went, the family followed for the Friday get-together. In spring she would retire for a few weeks to her country house, and a cortege of cars would make the two-hour drive on Fridays to join her for the day. We were rewarded with farm treats of fresh clotted cream and buttery pastry, and took long walks in the orchards. The summers she spent in her rambling, humid villa on the Corniche facing the sea in Alexandria.

Among her grandchildren, Nanou had a weakness for boys in general, and among the girls, for the prettiest, but she spoilt us all. "Love," she would say, "is like water," meaning that love flows from the older to the younger, and not vice versa, just as water flows downhill and not up. But it was a long time later that I understood what she meant, and it was only after she died that I learned from her the secret to summoning a spirit.

My first attempt at a séance happened when I was expecting my first baby; I had been living in London at the time but had gone home to Egypt to recover from severe morning sickness. It was during Ramadan, and my cousins and I were lounging around idly at Nanou's one night, when it occurred to us that it would be entertaining to bring in a spirit medium. Nanou's cook humored us by sending for a man who had a reputation for being able to call random spirits into his presence. He turned out to be a sharp-eyed, scruffy-bearded fellow who right away lost some of his credibility when my cousin Hala tested his psychic powers. "Is Nadia expecting a boy or a girl?" she asked.

He looked from one to the other of the group of girls; I was only four months pregnant and still flat as pita bread.

"Which one of you is Nadia?" he blurted. Then, to cover his confusion, he intoned, "Knowledge of the womb is hidden knowledge."

We went ahead gamely, following the medium's instructions to set up a table covered with a cloth in the middle of the salon and to draw chairs all around it. He put down a basket in the middle of the table, to receive the spirit, presumably, and a pencil and paper, which would write automatically of their own accord to record the answers the spirit would give to our questions. We argued among us about whose spirit we should try to conjure. Our recently deceased uncle, Nanou's second son, was the only relative of ours who had passed to the other side, but none of us had been close to him. That, I sensed, would be an obstacle; why would a spirit brave the great divide to answer a summons from a voice he had hardly known in life?

We turned off all the lights, sat down in a circle, and held hands, the excitement building in spite of our skepticism. Just then the door opened briskly and Nanou walked in. "What's this? A séance? Well, if you want to amuse yourselves, that's fine, but not you, Nadia; you come out with me right now."

"But Nanou," I wailed, "it's just for fun. You don't really believe in spirits, do you?"

"But you can scare yourself into miscarrying or harming that baby. You come with me right now."

It's one of the disappointments in my life that I never did get to attend the spirit séance. Later my cousins swore that the basket levitated, the tablecloth floated around the room, the pencil wrote of its own volition, and the windows slammed spontaneously. Knowing them, I was sure they exaggerated wildly to make me envious. Today I have had my own experiences of the intractably inexplicable, and I cannot afford to be as dismissive.

I left for England soon after that séance manqué and came back, months later, to have my baby in Cairo. When I went to the hospital to deliver, Nanou was there. I had a very long and difficult labor, and my poor mother climbed to the highest floor of the hospital building to be out of earshot of my screams. When I recovered from the anesthesia, however, I bounced back quickly. I sat up in my hospital bed and announced, before the assembled relatives, that I was hungry. Nanou hushed me, scandalized.

"What will your in-laws think!" she hissed in my ear. "You sound like a fellaha who delivers in the field and goes home with her baby in a basket. You're supposed to be all washed out after the terrible ordeal you've been through. Just lie quietly till everyone's gone, and I promise I'll send the driver to get you anything you want. Almond macaroons from Lappas? You love those, and it's good for the milk."

"And pistachio Turkish delight," I whispered back. "Oh, and Nanou, candied chestnuts from Groppi."

Nanou lived to see the rest of her grandchildren marry and many of her great-grandchildren born; she lived to see all of her daughters widowed or divorced; she was to mediate the estrangement between two of her sons; she was to suffer through the long, harrowing illness of a third son only to lose him in the end. As the years took their toll on her, she took to her bed for most of the day, and tended to listen more than to speak, but her mental acuity remained undiminished.

The family still gathered around her table on Fridays, and she still made the effort to have her cook prepare everyone's favorite dish. My father's favorite dessert was *Om Ali*, layers of pastry baked in cream with raisins and nuts. On Fridays at her house, it was invariably on the dessert buffet along with the other desserts. Nanou loved my father more as a son than a son-in-law. When he passed away, five years before her own death, she was inconsolable. I left for the States for good shortly after that. The first time I came back to Cairo to visit, and came to Friday dinner at Nanou's, I looked at the laden dessert buffet and unthinkingly remarked that there was no Om Ali.

"That was your father's favorite," she replied reproachfully. "We don't make it in this house any more."

And that is how I knew when Nanou died, although I was in the States and no one told me. I had a dream that Nanou and my father were eating Om Ali, and I woke up crying, because I knew, in my heart. I started crying even before I called home and asked about Nanou, and before I heard the fatal words: "May the rest of her life prolong yours."

I have no explanation for this; I only know I dreamed of my father after his death, and of Nanou after hers, even though I did not know she was dead. Those were the only times. Perhaps, if you are a person who is not particularly permeable to the spirit world, it takes great love for those departed to reach you in a vision. The secret to conjuring a spirit is love. It takes great love, on *both* sides of the ultimate divide, even if love is like water.

See Alexandria and Die

Alexandria. The saltiness of the sea breeze wafting off the marshes miles before the city came into view. The jangling of the trolley as it crossed the downtown. The whooshing sound of the waves dashing against the breakers long before the Corniche came into view around the bend. Finally, the first glimpse of the gray-green sea glinting under the blinding sun. The flavor of ripe mangoes and lemon ice granita on the tip of my memory. The promise of three months of vacation, three months of beach and books, three months surrounded by a gaggle of cousins.

We were summer people, but when I was young, we rented a small villa, a few blocks inland, away from the bustle of the Corniche, the main thoroughfare that wound along the bay. Every summer, at the beginning of June, we would pack a truck full of household linens, pots and pans, toys and books, and head out in a cortege from Cairo to Alex. My father drove the car, with my mother beside him, and my brother, our elderly governess, and I in the back. Ali the driver drove the rental truck, with Hassan the cook beside him; the suffragi and the maid came up on the train. We usually took the desert road, rather than the slower country road, and stopped once during the three-and-one-half-hour trip at the Rest House, which served delicious cheese pastries called *börek*. Once we arrived in Alexandria, my mother would supervise the unpacking and dusting, and by evening sheets would be on the beds, our clothes would be in the closets, and the first meal would be cooked in the kitchen.

In the mornings my parents slept late, and Madame Hélène, our governess, had instructions to keep us occupied and out of the way in the early hours. She took us for long walks along the boardwalk of the Corniche, where my brother would buy bait from the fishermen on the pier. We stopped at a stand where a man dropped small balls of fresh dough into hot oil, then dipped them into syrup, to make the crisp, sticky balls called "judge's mouthful," which he served in a paper cone. The governess claimed that it was safe to buy them early in the morning when the oil was fresh.

Around ten in the morning we set off in the car for the beach, driving the length of the Corniche to the tip of the bay. There loomed the Montazah Palace, the summer resort of the Khedives of Egypt before the revolution, a vast walled compound of beaches and gardens. After the overthrow of the monarchy, private cabanas for day use were built on the beaches within the grounds, beaches with names like Isis and Aida.

Semiramis Beach, where we had our cabana, was a small bay half encircled by a long pier tipped with a lighthouse. By the time children were nine, we were expected to be able to swim to the lighthouse and back, and parental supervision of our swimming came to an end. In retrospect, it surprises me that our parents, so overprotective in most respects, were so blessedly casual about our swimming. There were no sharks in that part of the Mediterranean, but debilitating cramp or fatigue were hazards they do not seem to have considered, nor the risk of getting run over by one of the motorboats pounding through the waves.

One time I had swum halfway to the lighthouse when a severe cramp immobilized my leg. I paddled around to face the shore and counted the rows of cabanas to pinpoint ours. I could make out two figures sitting in the little balcony, and waved frantically for help. They waved back. It never occurred to them that I could be in trouble. Luckily a cousin was swimming within earshot of my shouts and came to my rescue. Naturally, neither of us breathed a word of this incident, for fear our liberty in the water would be curtailed.

I was the poorest swimmer in the bunch of cousins, and also the one prone to sunburn, so I invariably spent the first few days at the beach in agony, covered with Nivea cream and yogurt to soothe my raw red skin. We spent three hours in the water at midday, while the adults took short dips. The mothers modestly wore a towel robe till they were practically in the water before slipping it off and handing it to one of us to carry back to a chair under the umbrella.

In the early afternoon we headed home for lunch and a siesta, and then we went to the Beau Rivage Hotel tea garden to feed the goldfish. Later in the evening we might go to San Giovanni's on the waterfront for a fish dinner, or downtown to Glimonopoli for water ices. Several times a week we went to the San Stefano Hotel to the open-air cinema to watch the triple feature; the younger children were sent home before the third, "grown-up" film.

But long before I was old enough to stay up even for the second feature, our lifestyle changed dramatically because of the sequestration decrees enacted against our family and others in the early sixties. At the time, I was told nothing of this situation, only that we would have to give up our summers in Alexandria and the three months in a rented villa. My mother claimed that the routine of picking up and setting up house in Alexandria every summer was exhausting, and no vacation for her, and that she preferred to go to the San Stefano Hotel for a short period instead. My brother and I were resentful. Now that I know the real reason, I see she had wanted to shield us from the truth about our altered circumstances, but I question her lack of faith in our maturity.

On the bright side, from the vantage point of our hotel room at the San Stefano, we could see the cinema for free, and all three features to boot.

The last time I saw Alexandria I was nineteen and it was early September, and almost all the summer people had gone back to Cairo. I had stayed behind with my grandmother in her rambling three-story house right on the Corniche in Laurent, so battered by the wind and the salt spray that over the years the walls had been worn into a honeycomb by the humidity. But Nanou's summer house was magical to me, teeming as it did in season with a bevy of cousins.

But that September when I stayed behind with Nanou and two cousins close to my age, Hala and Chazli, we had the rambling old house to ourselves, except for Grandmother's driver's daughter. Nanou had invited her to spend a few days in Alex and stressed that we were to be especially kind to the girl. She was in poor health and this trip was a special treat for her. She had never been anywhere outside of Cairo and had never seen the sea or even a lake.

"If I could only see Alexandria, I'd die happy the next day," she had reportedly told her father.

We drove to the beach the next morning, the three of us cousins jostling in the back seat, Hala between her brother Chazli and me. The chauffeur's daughter huddled in the front passenger seat next to her father, *Osta* Yunis, as we called him. Her name was Hanna, and she was a thin, dark girl in her early twenties, too shy to speak a word or do more than nod when spoken to as we wound our way along the Corniche. Traffic was light and the many small shops selling beach balls and inflatable rafts had an end-of-season look about them. The roast corn vendors on the boardwalk fanned their embers with a despondent air. But the weather was still very mild; green flags, rather than black, fluttered over the breakers.

"The green flags are flying today, so that means the water is calm, you know, Hanna," my cousin Hala ventured. "You can go for a dip if you like."

The girl looked embarrassed. It occurred to me that she wouldn't know how to swim.

"You might want to try to just wade in up to your knees or so," I suggested.

Hanna mumbled something noncommittal.

"She probably doesn't have a swimsuit," Chazli pointed out, in English.

"That's no problem! I'll buy her one." I leaned forward to speak to the driver in Arabic. "Osta Yunis, would you stop at the next shop that sells beach things?"

"But it's almost time for the Friday prayer, I can hear the muezzin now," he protested. "The shops are shutting down for the prayer already."

"But we might find one still open, if we hurry. How about that one at the corner? The shutter isn't down yet and it has some swimsuits hanging in the window. Hanna, we'll get you a swimsuit, that way you can swim today, okay?"

But by the time we pulled out of traffic and drew up to the tiny kiosks with beach balls and wood paddles and swimsuits hanging in front of the door, the shopkeepers had all put down their shutters.

"It's all right, Hanna," I decided suddenly. "You can have my swimsuit. I wasn't really planning to swim today anyway. And it's getting too small for me anyhow," I added quickly to hush her mumbled protests. "I couldn't have worn it another season, really. It's yours to keep." The swimsuit was only a little tight and it was my favorite, with its pink angelfish motif, so I felt particularly pleased with my gesture. I don't know why, but I just felt she might not get another chance to go for a swim. Whenever I think back on that morning, I remind myself of the Islamic injunction "Deeds are judged by the intention."

Yunis dropped us off at the cabana in Montazah and hurried off to the mosque to join in what was left of Friday prayers. Then he went back to Laurent to run errands for Nanou; we would spend the day at the beach and he would come back to fetch us later. I gave the pink angelfish swimsuit to Hanna and curled up on one of the rattan chairs on the balcony to read. Hala and Chazli swam out to the lighthouse and back. Then Hala came back to shower while Chazli took the paddleboard and paddled around the bay, waiting for his turn. We no longer spent three hours in the water. There were days when I did not even take a dip; it seemed like too much trouble to blow-dry my long hair straight. At the tail end of summer, at the tail end of adolescence, we were tired of both.

That day we had lunch at the cabana, unpacking the pic-nic that Nanou's cook had carefully packed for us. I never saw Hanna eat the lunch I served her; she must have put it aside and eaten it out of sight later. I wrapped the leftovers and gave them to one of the Montazah caretakers. Dressed in white fishermen's hats, navy jerseys, and pants rolled up over the knee, their job was to rake the beach and put away the parasols and paddleboards.

By late afternoon, when the heat set in, we let down the awning over the little balcony in front of the cabana and hooked the door open to create a draft. We lolled around on the cushions of the rattan furniture on the balcony, alter-nately reading and dozing. I remember the feel of those sun-bleached green cushions, always a little damp, stained where we had sat down in wet swimsuits, gritty with the sand encrusted in the white piping. The strange thing about memory is that it's like a palimpsest. If nothing overwrites it, it remains perfectly preserved.

There is another detail I remember from that afternoon, one I probably would not recall if what happened later that day had not fixed it in my memory. I remember I was read-ing one of the books of *The Alexandria Quartet,* and that I was horrified at the passage where Clea is trapped under-water and her lover, to save her from drowning, chops off her hand to free her. But the familiar sea in front of me held no terrors.

That afternoon, just before it was time to head back, I felt like going for a walk on my own. The sun was setting and the beach was deserted. In the distance I saw a catama-ran skimming the water, headed for shore. It belonged to a French couple; I had heard them talking earlier. A single swimmer bobbed in the foreground. I thought I could make out the swim cap and goggles of Doctor Wahbi, our neighbor two cabanas down. He was splashing toward the shore, snorting and blowing like a walrus.

I reached the pier and walked all the way to its tip, then walked back again and down the beach toward our cabana. The sun had set and the sky was streaked with mauve and gold. The catamaran had come on shore and was lying on its side on the dune. I could make out some people huddled around something.

I hurried toward them. I could hear the Frenchwoman crying and saw her straighten up and turn away from whatever lay there on the sand. Her companion took her in his arms, trying to calm her. Then I saw Dr. Wahbi as he got up off his knees, the fleshy folds of his chest and belly wobbling. He had taken off his goggles and his eyes were bloodshot from the salt water.

"Dr. Wahbi? It's Nadia." I knew he might not recognize me without his glasses. "What's wrong?"

He put out his arm to stop me from coming any closer.

"Don't look, child. It's a terrible thing, poor girl. I tried, but it was too late. There was nothing I could do. I don't know who it is, I don't think I've ever seen her before, but without my glasses . . . "

I took two steps closer and looked. There was a body lying prone on the sand. A body in a pink angelfish swimsuit. I stifled a scream.

"That's Hanna!"

"Who?"

"I know who it is! That's Hanna! The chauffeur's daughter. What's wrong with her? What happened?"

The French couple had seen the girl first, as they had surfed to shore. They had seen someone floating face down in two feet of water. At first they had thought she was holding her breath and then they had realized she was drowned and had pulled her up the beach. Their shouts for help had brought Dr. Wahbi rushing out of the water. He had tried to resuscitate the girl but it was too late.

Dr. Wahbi headed to his cabana to call an ambulance. It was rapidly getting dark and a cool breeze was blowing. Lights were coming on in one or two cabanas. A handful of people started to trickle down the beach and gather at a distance as word of mouth spread about a drowning.

Chazli came running. He was heading straight for the figure on the sand. I called him and he spun around. When he saw me he let out a breath as if he'd been punched in the stomach.

"Nadia! They said a girl drowned on the beach—the swimsuit—I thought it was you! Is it poor Hanna? What happened?"

He came and stood by me. I pressed my arms under my chest, feeling sick.

A small crowd had gathered; people shook their heads and muttered the usual formulas. "Take refuge in the Lord." "There is no power but Allah's." "We are his and to him we return." The Frenchwoman was led away by her companion, crying noisily.

I glanced at the body, at the dark hairs gleaming on the skinny legs. Poor Hanna had been so shy, she would hate to be exposed in her unprepared half-nakedness. I went and stood in front of her to shield her from the stares of onlookers. Chazli took off his shirt and covered her legs.

Dr. Wahbi came back, wearing his glasses. He had a towel over his shoulders and one in his hand, which he spread over the body in the angelfish swimsuit.

"It's my fault," I moaned. "If I hadn't given her the swimsuit—I should have known she couldn't swim . . . "

"She didn't try to swim, child," Dr. Wahbi put a hand on my shoulder. "She was in two feet of water, barely wading. She didn't drown at all. She had a heart attack. Then she fell into the water."

"But why did she have a heart attack? I mean, she was young . . . "

"Nanou said she was sickly, remember," Chazli pointed out.

"Yes, well, without knowing her medical history, I can only guess." Dr. Wahbi took off his glasses and rubbed his red eyes. "I don't know, Nadia. Sudden heart failure is uncommon, but it happens. Maybe the shock of the water. It's sad. It's very sad."

"If only someone had seen her. If only there'd been someone on the beach . . . " Chazli began.

"But Chazli, don't you see, she waited till she made sure there was no one there! She's so shy, she wouldn't have wanted anyone to see her."

The ambulance arrived and we fumbled in our pockets for money to tip the drivers. Dr. Wahbi got in the van with Hanna.

"You said she was the chauffeur's daughter?" he called to us. "Someone had better notify her father."

"Oh my God, yes! Osta Yunis drove back to the house because Nanou needed him. He was supposed to come fetch us around now."

"I'll call Nanou and tell her not to send him." Chazli headed for the cabana. "We'll take a taxi home. Then we'll tell Nanou to break the news to him."

As it turned out Yunis took it very philosophically.

"She's always been so sickly, my Hanna. I always knew I would never see her live to be a bride. But she was so happy, when we came to Alexandria, when she saw the sea. It was like a dream come true. Her heart just burst."

☙☙The next summer I married and left for Europe, and didn't go back to Alexandria for decades. For me it was never the same again. I had lost my sense of security in the familiar waters of childhood; I had lost my innocence about good intentions; I had seen death for the first time, where and when I least expected it. An irrational sense of guilt nagged me whenever I remembered Alexandria, and Hanna: the notion that what had lain in wait for the pink angelfish swimsuit in the calm turquoise waters that afternoon had been intended for me, not her.

But Alexandria, that grand old lady of the glorious past and the cosmopolitan pretensions, was already on the decline the last time I left her. By then the beaches were far from pristine; black tar clung to our heels when we went for a walk on the sand and we kept a bottle of kerosene in the cabana to wipe our feet clean. The surf washed up strands of rubbish raked up daily by the Montazah caretakers. As the Corniche become more crowded, Alexandria was abandoned, little by little, for the coast to the west of it. Over the next two decades, spanking new beach resorts sprang up westward all the way to Sidi Abdel Rahman and beyond. Alexandria was finally abandoned by summer people like us.

ଛଡ଼But today as I approach by car, I feel like one of the ancient Arab poets who, according to the convention of classical Arabic poetry, begin each epic with a sorrowful visit to old haunting grounds. I see a sign flash by: Alexandria 20 Kilometers. It is in Greek as well as Arabic, and that is new; a reminder that this is the one true Alexandria, of the many eponymous cities that Alexander the Great strewed in his restless wake, the one metropolis that flourished and sparkled in the sun while its sixteen sisters faded in its shadow, from Kandahar to Iskenderun.

This evening as I walk along the Corniche I breathe in the invigorating breeze blowing off the sea as the sun sets in a glory of purple. There are women in headscarves everywhere now, nearly as ubiquitous as in Cairo, and there is an air of bustle and new construction. The elegant old villas are long gone, including my grandmother's dear, damp house in Laurent, and replaced by tall buildings; new hotels are springing up, and old ones refurbished. Excavation teams are uncovering the ruins of Cleopatra's palace lying on the sea floor of the bay. The gleaming hemisphere of a new library looms low over the skyline, in homage to the great library of Alexandria that was the envy of the world when Plutarch wrote history.

Driving along the Corniche from the fifteenth-century Qait Bey Fort at the tip of the bay to Montazah Palace at the other end, with the palm trees swaying in the breeze, and a willing imagination, it almost reminds me of Nice. I go for a walk around the Montazah grounds and find the drowned ruins of President Sadat's summer villa; the guards let me look around. I stay at the Salamlek Hotel, which was once a little folly the Khedive built for his Austrian mistress. From my hotel window I look out over the small bay of Semiramis Beach; I count the rows of cabanas and pinpoint the one that used to be mine.

Driving back down the Corniche, I see a newly erected statue of Alexander the Great, harking far back to the city's Ptolemaic heyday, before Cleopatra's fleet burned in the bay; before the Romans dug the maze of catacombs that lurks underground; before the Mamluks erected Qait Bey Fort over the ruins of the Pharos; before the Khedives built the Montazah Palace; before it became Lawrence Durrell's Alexandria; before it was mine.

The Worst-Case Scenario

"I can't sleep. I'm so worried. What if I fail? What if I don't do well on my exams?"

It was about two o'clock after midnight of a night in June, and in six hours I would be sitting for the first of a week-long series of exams, the dread General Certificate of Secondary Studies—Secondary General for short—that would decide my academic future. I was sixteen, but I didn't hesitate to wake my parents at two o'clock in the morning, knocking on the door that closed off their two-bedroom suite. My parents had separate bedrooms but my mother only used hers during the day, to dress and do bills and chat on the phone. They locked the door to their suite at night, but I knew I could knock any time I couldn't sleep; my mother would open the door for me, then tumble back into bed while my father, a fellow insomniac, would ask me what was wrong.

"I can't sleep. I'm so worried. What if I fail? What if I don't do well on my exams?"

"Take a Valium pill from the medicine cabinet," Mama mumbled into her pillow, with a layperson's insouciance about dispensing medications.

"Come on, let's go out on the verandah and let your mother go back to sleep," my father countered as he got out of bed.

44

We strolled back and forth on the verandah in the faint moonlight; the temperature had dropped to a merely uncomfortable 97 degrees from an intolerable daytime high of 108; tomorrow was predicted to be another scorcher. For the first time in my life, I would be leaving my private English-language school for girls, to join hundreds of thousands of Egyptian secondary students in sweltering university halls. Twelve years of schooling would ride entirely on the results of one week of exams. Each exam was followed by a ten-minute break, followed by another three-hour exam. This schedule went on for one brutal week. Every year dozens of students, usually girls, fainted or threw up from heat and nerves, and a handful of students, usually boys, committed suicide from pressure or disappointment.

"What if I don't do well?" I fretted as I walked back and forth with my father on the verandah that night.

"Let's think this through for a minute. What's the worst-case scenario?"

"That I won't do well enough on my exams to get the cumulative score I need to be accepted at the Faculty of Politics."

"In that case, you won't get into Politics, to which you are only applying to please me, and you will get your second choice, English Literature, and please yourself."

It was true that it was my father who had influenced me away from English Lit to Politics. "The situation is so bad in this country, Nadia habibti. You should plan on leaving here as soon as you can, for graduate school. A degree in English would be worthless to you in Europe. But a degree in Economics or Politics is a transferable commodity."

"But what if I don't even do well enough to get accepted into English Lit?" I persisted, mostly for argument's sake.

"In that case," my father humored me, "you won't go to college at all, we'll marry you off early."

"But what if no one proposes to marry me?"

"Then you'll stay home, and keep your father company! Now go back to bed and get some sleep. Just remember that the worst-case scenario isn't so bad."

He had understood, knowing me as he did, that what I needed from him was an advance dispensation in the event that I disappoint him.

A month later, when my test scores came back, I was in a quandary. My father had given me his word that if I scored high enough for Politics, it would still be up to me to choose English Lit. And I knew he meant it. I had learned just how much he valued keeping his word only a few months earlier.

It was during the spring of 1968, nearly a year after Egypt's shocking defeat in the Six-Day War, when it became apparent that the postwar promises of reform were not materializing. Students at Cairo University spontaneously turned out into the streets in mass demonstrations unprecedented under the Nasser regime. Perhaps it was a wind of rebellion in the air that year that blew across the Mediterranean and caught up young people everywhere in its slipstream: Cairo had its 1968, just as Paris and Prague did. Students cut classes, took to the streets, waved protest banners, and organized sit-ins.

The security police immediately locked down the bridges across the Nile, cutting off the university campus in Giza from the rest of Cairo; tear gas was used to disrupt the demonstrations and students were arrested right and left. The self-contained campus of the Engineering School was the logical choice for a sit-in because it had its own power generators. My brother was a student in engineering at the time, and when he was hours late coming home we were worried.

He finally turned up, dusty from walking home part of the way over the road-blocked bridges, but excited, even elated.

"The students organizing the sit-in wouldn't let anyone leave; they said we all needed to stick together. But I told them I had to go home to check on my family and let them know I was all right," he explained between gulps of mango juice. "I gave them my word I would come back and they made an exception for me. They're planning on holding out as long as the water and power do." He started to get up. "I'd better go; I promised to be back before it gets dark."

"You can't go back!" my mother exclaimed. "Don't you see, it's different for you. When the students get arrested, the others will be released soon enough. But you they'll hold, because of your family name. They'll accuse you of being the ringleader, they'll make an example of you. All they want is an excuse to claim these demonstrations are a conspiracy of the 'feudalists' and the enemies of the people. Don't you see? You'll be playing right into their hands. You simply can't go back."

"But I gave my word!"

"Listen to me. It's not just yourself you are putting at risk here. They'll come after your father, your uncles. They might even let you go, but they'll arrest your father."

This was a blow beneath the belt; for the first time, my brother wavered. We looked at my father, who had been silent. He took a long pull on his pipe. I had never seen him so conflicted.

"A man is only as good as his word," he finally said. "If you gave your word that you would go back, you must."

My brother went back. My father and I didn't even bother to go to bed; we stayed up in the verandah and tried to while away the time talking, as we often did. Nothing was taboo in our open-ended discussions, not even religion. I remember asking him what proof there was that the Quran was truly divine revelation channeled through the prophet and not the expression of the genius of an extraordinarily gifted poet/philosopher. My mother, breezing through at that moment, caught the tail end of the conversation, as she tended to do, and tossed over her shoulder authoritatively, "We know Muhammad was a true prophet because it says so in the Quran." She sailed away, leaving my father and me slack-jawed at her breathtaking lapse in logic. To be fair, it probably hit her by the time she reached the top of the stairs, if she gave it any thought. But Mama believed that religion, like marriage, required a blind leap of faith and that too much deliberating about either could only lead to doubt and damnation.

None of us slept that night, until my brother came back early in the morning, after the students dispersed of their own accord. Then we all went to bed in broad daylight.

By the time I started college that fall, the campus was subdued again. I had enrolled at the Faculty of Politics after all, and had no regrets, but my first day on campus was traumatic. Coming from my private, sheltered girls' school, I was unprepared, at sixteen, for the sheer size of the Cairo University campus and for the throngs of students of both sexes and all backgrounds. My very first day, a student detached himself from a group who had been whispering at my approach; he blocked my way as I headed for class.

"I know you had nothing to do personally with the injustices perpetrated by the feudalists and capitalists before the Revolution, of course, you weren't around, but I want to hear how you justify what people like your family did."

Two things stood out about him: his crew-cut blond hair, because it is rare in Egyptians; and one single, very long nail, on the little finger of his right hand, in the manner of apprentice auto mechanics. The group of students in the corner were straining their ears to hear our exchange. I remember thinking that if they smelled blood, if I let them see that I was shaken, I would never be able to set foot on campus again. They had already made up their minds about me; they mistook the awkwardness of a sheltered upbringing for snobbishness. That would have to be my defense.

"What makes you think," I asked coldly, "that I feel the need to justify anything to you? I don't know you." I spun on my heel and walked away. No one bothered me again. I surprised myself that day.

I was married the month I graduated from college, and left immediately for London. Years later, when I came back from England, Papa's health had deteriorated alarmingly.

My first son was about four at the time, a whirlwind of a boy who ran everyone ragged, especially at bath time: one minute he would be splashing happily in the tub, and the next, with a wild whoop, he would leap out, bang through the door, and streak like quicksilver down the long corridor, across the hall at the top of the stairs, through the family room where we watched television, and out to the verandah where he knew my father had taken up his evening watch. By the time I caught up with him, the little monkey would be panting and grinning in my father's lap, his skinny ribcage shielded by my father's large hands.

"Leave him be, Nadia, leave him be, I have precious little time with him as it is."

"But Papa, he always does this, and his hair will get tangled if I don't comb it while it's wet, and it's late for his bedtime!"

"Leave him be, habibti, you did the same, you know, at his age."

And that would shame me into wrapping a towel around the little imp and leaving them together on the verandah. My son's high voice would start up right away: "Grandpa, how many stars are there? Why can't we see them all at once? Where do the others go? Why? Why not? Why?"

I didn't admit to myself that the real reason I let it go was that I sensed what little time we had left with my father. He had had heart attacks alarmingly often over the past few years, but he always seemed to recover. After the last one, though, he sent for my brother from London, and sat down with him for days sorting through piles of worn manila folders and boxes of faded, dog-eared papers, the very oldest in the original French, but mostly in Arabic: titles to properties, court documents, bank statements, and endless files labeled "Sequestration Authority." He was intent on organizing all the paperwork to leave his children in a position to reclaim their confiscated inheritance from the state after his death. At first Papa insisted I sit down with him and my brother and pay attention, but trying to concentrate on those documents gave me a headache. He let me off, after a while; in retrospect, I think he understood, better than I did, that I was hanging onto my denial for as long as I could.

One evening, I can't remember why, Papa spoke sharply to my brother and me. This was so rare, coming from him, that we were stricken with remorse. A few minutes later he called us to his room. "It's my illness," he apologized; "it makes me irritable. In this final stage, it has that effect." The look in his eyes followed his statement with a question.

I took both his hands in mine and locked my eyes on his. "You're not irritable, Papa," I insisted. "You're not irritable. You're not."

My brother did not do much better. "I only wish you'd let yourself lose your temper with us sometimes," he said. "We'd feel better." We both failed my father that day: he had the right to expect his adult son and daughter to let him speak of the death that stared him in the face, and instead we had reacted with the self-protective denial of children.

Whatever we knew or chose not to admit to ourselves about my father's condition, it was a shock when the last massive coronary took him away. I remember my mother pleading with the doctor, "Anything but that, anything but that," as if she were trying to strike a bargain, and so she was—but not with the doctor. She was bargaining with God, but sometimes even blind faith cannot save us from the worst-case scenario, it can only help us to bear it.

It makes me sad to think that my first son was the only one of his grandchildren my father lived to see. That son, grown up now, has nothing of his grandfather's appearance or temperament, and hardly remembers him, or so I thought. The last time I went to visit my son in London, we walked home after dinner at his favorite Indian restaurant in Kensington. It was an exceptionally balmy evening, the sky still awash in pale lingering light. We strolled along, he with his hands in the pockets of his suit, making an effort to rein in his long stride to accommodate my shorter steps. The whirlwind boy has grown into a man who is not much of a talker, but he can be a good listener. I found myself telling him about a particular situation that was preoccupying me at the time.

"Mummy," he said, when I was done fretting, "let's think this through for a minute. Bottom line, what's the worst-case scenario here?"

I told him.

"Well then, can you live with it?"

I considered that for a moment. "I suppose I can."

"Then don't sweat it. If you can live with your worst-case scenario, then don't sweat it."

I stared, bemused, at my newly wise son, wondering why the words had a familiar ring. And then I remembered. Walking back and forth on the verandah with my father the night before my Secondary General exam.

"I can't sleep. What if I don't do well?"

And my father's voice. "Let's think this through for a minute. What's the worst-case scenario?"

The Haggana

Around ten o'clock that morning I woke to the sound of the doorbell. I slipped on my dressing gown and cracked open the door of the apartment. Ibrahim the doorkeeper stood there with a girl of about sixteen, wearing a small black kerchief knotted over tight chestnut braids and clutching a knapsack. She shot me a look out of bright hazel eyes, then fixed her gaze on her pink plastic slippers. She had the ram-rod posture of country women trained to balance heavy jars of water on their heads.

Ibrahim cleared his throat and began to speak in his most deliberate Nubian manner. "*Ya Sitt,* this girl is from the country and has no place to stay. She would be glad to work for room and board and whatever you want to give her. We were hoping you could use her help around the apartment while you're in Cairo. Just till I find a permanent situation for her."

It had occurred to me that I needed some help with the housekeeping, but it seemed too much trouble to find a maid for the few weeks I would be in Cairo, that winter in the early nineties. But the weeks might stretch into months; this temporary arrangement could work out well. Still, I hesitated. Over the long years of living abroad I had lost the habit of live-in household help, and I wasn't sure I was ready to trade my privacy for the convenience. On the other hand this poor girl had no place to stay. Whatever her circumstances, hers must be a true hard-luck story to have won the sympathy of the dour old doorkeeper.

"What's your name?" I asked.

"Aisha, Sitt."

"All right, Aisha, come on in. I'll show you the kitchen."

Aisha seemed to be clean and very willing, but obviously new to domestic service and to urban life. Right away, unasked, she took it into her head to wash the hallway floor. Before I could stop her, she had slopped a bucket of sudsy water over the polished parquet. Several of the intricate chevron-patterned squares came loose.

❧❧In the mornings now I woke to the sound of Aisha opening all the windows to the noise and dust in the street. She slept in the laundry room on the roof but every morning she let herself in the kitchen door. With Aisha in the house there was always a restless swish of sound and motion in the background. First thing in the morning, she opened the windows, then she hung the mattresses and the rugs over the balcony railing and banged away at them with a bamboo duster, pausing every so often to engage in conversation with Ibrahim or the neighbor's maid passing by. Whenever she heard someone at the gate she rushed over to the kitchen window to see who it was. In the evenings, if I turned on the television, she would creep up to the doorway and peer in. I motioned to her and she quickly slipped into the room and sat cross-legged on the floor in front of the set, her face rapt in the flickering light of the screen.

One morning when I got up and went to the kitchen, Aisha greeted me with "Happy Mulid, Sitt!"

I remembered that it was the festival of the Prophet's birthday. "Good morning, and happy Mulid to you too. Tell me, Aisha, don't you have any relatives in Cairo you might want to visit for the Mulid?"

"No, Sitt, I have no one in Cairo."

The dog started barking. Aisha immediately stuck her head out of the window to satisfy her curiosity. To my surprise she dropped the duster and gave a little cry. She wiped her hands on her apron and rushed out of the kitchen. I heard her clattering down the spiral iron back stairs. A few minutes later she was back, tugging by the sleeve a young soldier in drab khaki. In the kitchen he held his cap in his hand and grinned shyly while Aisha chattered away at me.

"Sitt Nadia, this is my husband."

"I didn't know you were married, Aisha!"

"Oh yes, but he's a conscript, you see. He got leave today because it's the Mulid. May I go out with him, please, Sitt? I'll be back by morning, I promise."

"Of course, Aisha, you may go."

The next morning I got up and unlocked the kitchen door to get the morning paper. I found Aisha huddled on the doormat, fast asleep. She was clutching a doll made of painted sugar candy and dressed in pleated gold tissue paper. It was one of those dolls you see displayed, along with the equally garish candy horses, all over the sweet shops in the souk during the Mulid; little girls are given dolls, and boys are given horses.

Aisha turned out to be honest and reliable. Her husband came every Friday, her day off, to take her out, and on Saturday she came back by morning. She always brought me some token, a paper cone of roasted peanuts or a bunch of mint.

About a month after she started working for me, the doorbell rang one afternoon, shattering the calm of siesta time. Aisha was up on the roof hanging the wash on a line, so I opened the door. Ibrahim stood there with a square-shouldered man in army uniform; he had startling light gray eyes in a sun-scorched, unsmiling face. I recognized the insignia of the *Haggana,* the Egyptian desert patrol, on his uniform. I had seen the Haggana often along the coast near Alamein. At dusk they would appear out of nowhere, the camels loping along the wet white sand of the beach-front, the riders veiled against the desert wind, their rifles slung across their backs. Then they would vanish as silently as clouds over the sand dunes.

Ibrahim gave me to understand that the soldier was Aisha's brother. I didn't doubt it; they had the same coloring, unusual in Egyptians but fairly common in certain villages of the Delta where half the children running barefoot in the dust seem to be fair and hazel-eyed.

"He's come for his sister." There was something about Ibrahim's manner, regretful and resigned at the same time, that seemed ominous.

"Aisha will be down in a few minutes." I motioned for the man to come in. Ibrahim excused himself and left, leaving the door open behind him.

"Thank you, ma'am." The Haggana stood stiffly with his hands behind his back just inside the doorway. He spoke with only a trace of a country accent, unlike his sister. I tried to make conversation.

"So you're Aisha's brother? She hasn't really told me anything about her family. I'm glad to have her here, she's a great help. She's been very good about coming back on time after her days off. Her husband picks her up every Friday but she's always back by Saturday morning."

He said nothing but his eyes narrowed and a muscle in his temple twitched; the tension under his composure was suddenly unmistakable. It made me uneasy. Just then I thought I heard Aisha clattering down the iron service stairs from the roof. On impulse, I decided to stall the Haggana.

"Let me go see what's holding up Aisha." I moved in front of him and took hold of the doorknob. "Would you wait outside for a minute?" I tried to make it sound like the natural request of a conventional woman reluctant to let a strange man into her home while she was alone.

But he was not taken in. He hesitated, darting a look down the hallway and then back at me. I counted on his not daring to brush past me to get in, and moved toward him, drawing the door with me. He stepped back, momentarily off balance, and I shut the door in his face.

I hurried to the kitchen. Aisha was coming in the back door, humming through the clothespins in her mouth. She was carrying a big hamper of clean laundry.

"Aisha, your brother's here."

She dropped the hamper and clapped her hand over her mouth, looking around wild-eyed. "Where?"

"He's waiting outside the front door."

The girl started slapping her face. "Did you tell him I was here? I'm ruined! He'll kill me!"

"What on earth are you going on about? Calm down and tell me what's wrong. Aren't you glad to see your brother?"

"He'll kill me! Don't you see? My husband isn't really my husband—I mean he is before Allah, and he should have been my husband before the law, but my mother—Allah

forgive her, she's a hard woman! She must have sent for my
brother to look for me. What shall I do? I'm ruined! I might
as well kill myself, I won't go back with him, I won't!"

I made her sit down and drink some water while I tried
to question her. I was able to piece some sort of narrative
from her disjointed answers, interrupted by bouts of sob-
bing and rocking back and forth in her seat.

Aisha was the youngest of three pretty sisters, the belles
of their tiny village in the Delta. Their mother, a greedy
woman by Aisha's account, encouraged a succession of suitors to court her three daughters. When she had milked each
suitor in turn for as much as could be expected of the custom-
ary courtship gifts—a sheep, a gold bangle—she would break
off her daughter's engagement, freeing her to be courted by
another lovelorn dupe. The girls never exchanged more than a
few words with their suitors; needless to say, they were never
allowed to keep any of the gifts, nor were their wishes ever
consulted. As for the two older sisters, when the local supply
of swains was exhausted, they were married off to the highest
bidder, in both cases older, well-off farmers from neighboring
towns, able to afford the luxury of a second wife.

Aisha, the only one left at home, played her role obe-
diently until this last suitor, the young soldier. They fell in
love. When her mother decided his limited means had been
exhausted and that it was time to dismiss him, Aisha begged
and pleaded to be allowed to marry him. Her mother beat
her, locked her up, and forbade her ever to see him again.
The next time the young conscript, home on leave, came
calling, he found the door locked against him.

That night Aisha made her escape with her young lover.
Under cover of darkness they raced through the scorched

cornstalks while the village dogs howled in their wake. They ran till they flung themselves on the screeching train as it crawled through the fields, carrying peasants with wares to market in Cairo and Nubians on their long journey upcountry.

Once in Cairo, Aisha and her young suitor must have felt lost; they were far from home and had nowhere to go. They wandered around the leviathan of a metropolis for a few hours, but the soldier's leave was coming to an end and he had to report to barracks the next day. They stopped to wash at the courtyard fountain of a mosque. Desperate, they took the kindly-looking custodian into their confidence. He happened to know Ibrahim the doorkeeper, and asked him to find the girl a place to stay. So it was that Aisha showed up at my door that morning.

The soldier was stationed at the old Huckstep Barracks on the outskirts of Cairo, and whenever he could, he came to take Aisha out. They went to the amusement park and he bought her bags of roasted peanuts and jasmine blossom necklaces. At night they rocked themselves to sleep in one of the cars of the abandoned Ferris wheel. They never made love.

"But why didn't you get married?" I asked Aisha.

"I'm under sixteen, and besides, I don't have any papers, when I ran away I had nothing." She wiped her nose on the back of her hand. "But I won't go back, I'd rather die. I'll tell my brother I'm no longer a virgin; that way they won't be able to marry me off to someone else. They can't have a scandal in the village. They'll either have to let me marry my man or they'll have to kill me."

"Don't lie to your brother about that, it's the worst thing you could do. Besides, Aisha, don't you think you're overreacting?" Honor killings—that was a thing of the past, surely?

The girl looked at me as if I were naïve. "You don't understand. There can't be a scandal in the village. We're fellahin." She used the term for peasant in a sense I understood immediately: the fellahin were a byword for unforgiving mores, particularly where women's "honor" was concerned.

"All right, Aisha. Don't worry, we'll think of something."

I got up and walked over to the kitchen window. A man leaning against the wall by the back door caught my eye. He was wearing a Haggana uniform also; a friend of the brother's, presumably, guarding the back door. It would be no use trying to slip Aisha out that way. Besides, where could she go? Her brother had tracked her down once, he would find her again.

What could I do? Call the police? There was nothing for them to go on but the girl's fears. The Haggana had not done or said anything threatening. The girl was a minor; her brother had every right to insist on taking her home.

I called the most influential person I knew, my eldest uncle. He told me he would send over one of the junior lawyers he retained. An hour later the man arrived.

The lawyer argued and negotiated with the Haggana outside my door, but the soldier would not be budged. He insisted on taking his sister home. The lawyer drew up papers for him to sign, holding him responsible if anything untoward happened to the girl while she was in his charge. The Haggana signed everything, quickly and impassively, took poor sniveling Aisha and her few belongings, and left.

"Don't worry," the lawyer tried to reassure me, "I made him all but sign his life away."

But I doubted the Haggana had been taken in. He must have known there was no way to keep track of him or his sister once they left for their remote village in the Delta.

All night I didn't so much as try to sleep; I worried about Aisha. I had slipped her as much money as I had cash in the house, hoping that it might sweeten her mother's temper. I couldn't help feeling responsible, as if I had unwittingly betrayed her to her brother. I had been gone too long, I had lived abroad too long; I had failed to judge a situation that should have rung alarm bells from the start. I felt I didn't belong here, as if I spoke the language but didn't understand it.

Every culture has its transgressive lovers, its Romeo and Juliette, its Tristan and Isolde, its Qais and Laila, and they are doomed to be punished by the heavy hand of society wearing the mask of fate. But who chronicles the sad little romances of the poor and obscure? I kept wondering what would happen to little Aisha. I couldn't hope that she would be allowed to marry her shy young soldier. I imagined her married to a suitor of her mother's choice, surrounded by children, growing prematurely old in the way of country women who lead hard lives. In any case I didn't believe the Haggana would harm her—I only wished I knew for sure.

The Zawiya

Camelia is getting shampooed by one of the hairdresser's assistants, and I'm sitting with a towel wrapped around my head while the conditioner is supposed to work its magic. Hala is at the penultimate stage, waiting for Sayid, the salon owner, to personally do her blow-dry and "brushing."

It is curious how the coiffeur ritual, more than any other, makes me feel that I am slipping back into the familiar grooves of life in Cairo. There are certain lubricating rites of passage that ease the visiting expatriate back into her old self with a sigh of rediscovered comfort, like slipping on a perfectly worn pair of slippers. A visit to the coiffeur is one of them.

When Hala and Camelia and I were teenagers, the weekly visit to Sayid's busy three-room salon in Zamalek was a two-hour affair. We socialized and read magazines, studied, and sipped Turkish coffee, waiting to be passed from hand to hand, shampoo to deep condition to roller-set to blow-dry to the final "brush out," the culminating point at which we finally got the undivided attention of Sayid himself. In those days we all had long, lush hair that took hours to style fashionably stick-straight. Every month or so we had our tresses twisted into tight spirals along which a lighted match was passed to singe off the split ends. On New Year's Eve, we spent three hours getting elaborate chignons erected on our heads, and even then we weren't done:

we returned to the salon in the evening, all dressed up, for Sayid's *coup de peigne* and perhaps a final flourish like a silk flower to complement the dress.

Today reminds me of old times, except that there are only five customers in the salon, including the three of us. Camelia is talking to Hala and me over the sound of running water as the man massages his fingers into her lathered scalp. "But seriously, do you think those sconces are worth the price? How would they look in the foyer? Actually I'm thinking of them for Dina. I know there's no wedding date set yet, but still, I have all the furniture to buy—Ooh, that water is too hot, Ali! I mean Adel," she complains to the assistant.

"By all means, get them," Hala agrees, "as long as you like them. That way if Dina doesn't like them or there's no place for them in her apartment, you could always use them."

"Well, exactly. I don't know what kind of apartment the boy will provide—although his parents have been talking about building on a tract of land they have in one of the new compounds in the suburbs. One floor for each son and one for the parents. I do like the boy so much, but if his people don't come through with the right kind of apartment, and everything else they promised—I don't know. We might have to break off the engagement. What a headache this is, setting up a young couple. I do think it's harder being the bride's family and having all the trousseau and furniture to buy. As they say, you should marry your daughter to a Syrian and your son to an Egyptian." Camelia laughs but her daughter's engagement seems to be weighing on her mind.

Adel wraps her head in a pink towel and she sits up and moves into the chair next to me. "I suppose you don't have to worry about all that, Nadia, living in the States."

"Well, at least in Egypt the groom's family pays for the wedding. In the States it's the bride's, mostly."

"How old are your boys now? Do you have any photos?" Camelia stretches out a hand to the manicurist, a young woman in a headscarf, who has just set up her stool and tray in front of us. "Just a regular manicure today, Saniya, I don't have time for a French manicure."

Hala stands in front of the mirror, sucking in her tummy. She has grown quite chubby of late, and her short black hair lies flat in soft curls, emphasizing her full, round face and wide brown eyes. "So, Nadia, any photos?"

"I don't know if I have any recent photos of the boys, they've become so camera-shy. There's one with me and my younger one—snapshots at a Halloween party last year." I fish out my pocketbook and flip through it.

Sayid comes over to usher Hala to a chair; he hasn't changed much over the years, except for the proud references to "the engineer"—his son—and "the Doctora," his daughter, a Ph.D. in economics. He slides his fingers through Hala's short hair and flicks on the blow-dryer, wielding the round bristle brush in his other hand.

I fish out the photograph. Camelia cranes her neck, her hands temporarily incapacitated by the manicurist's attentions. I hold up the photo of me with my younger son, dressed for a party at a friend's house in Winston-Salem. Sherif towers over me in a Phantom of the Opera mask and cape. For my own costume I had recycled an old formal gown I had originally worn to a summer evening wedding in Egypt: a strapless, Empire-waisted, peach chiffon. For the Halloween party, I'd added long opera gloves, a satin wrap, and a fake tiara. The "costume" had been a great success that night.

"That's a pretty dress you're wearing," Camelia comments on the photo, "but you couldn't get away with something so bare here in Egypt."

Suddenly I remember the family wedding for which I'd had the dress made. "But I did wear it in Egypt! I wore it to Hala's wedding, and you were there, Camelia, we were all there, and you all thought it was lovely at the time."

"My wedding? Are you sure? It was twenty years ago! Let's see." Hala has caught the gist of the conversation in the intervals between the blasts from the blow-dryer.

I hand her the photo. "I'm positive. When you get home take out your wedding photo album and look through it. I must be in some of the pictures."

"You would be, of course. Aren't you lucky that you're still the same size you were twenty years ago? I couldn't get into any of my clothes from back then!" She hands the photo back to me.

"Sayid, do you remember styling my hair for my wedding?" I ask him. "What an elaborate do! Like a wedding cake."

"Who could forget, you were a beautiful bride," he answers gallantly. "A handsome couple! Everyone remarked on it."

I don't mention my divorce to Sayid, of course, but Camelia and Hala shoot sympathetic glances in my direction.

Adel wraps a cape around my shoulders and guides me to a sink to rinse out my hair. Meanwhile Sayid is done with Hala and is blow-drying Camelia's chin-length, smooth brown hair.

When she is ready she goes to the till to pay, slipping tips into the pockets of Adel and Saniya on her way back.

She stands in front of the mirror and fishes out a sheer scarf and plays with it, loosely draping it over her hair, tossing one end of it over her shoulder. She turns her head this way and that in the mirror coquettishly. The scarf sets off her hazel eyes and oval face to advantage.

"What do you think, girls?" She turns to Hala and me. "What would you think if I started wearing hijab? Just a loose scarf like this, I mean, not one of those strict nun-like jobs."

"Don't even think about it." I shake my head and wince as my wet hair snags on Adel's comb. "Besides, think how hot you'd be in summer."

"What's this, out of the blue?" Hala asks.

"Oh, it's just that I'm not getting any younger, and since I came back from Hajj this year, I've been thinking I should do it. But Hazem is completely against it, and I don't think a wife should go against her husband's wishes, do you? Of course Doctora Nahed says that a woman's duty to God comes before her husband's wishes, but how would she know what kind of relationship I have with my husband? You know how sweet Hazem is, he wouldn't intentionally do anything to displease me, so how can I go against his wishes? Besides, he has so many European clients, and we go out with them often, what would they think?"

"Who's this Doctora Nahed?"

"She's the preacher at our Koranic study circle. Hala comes sometimes."

"That's right. Nadia, you might remember her. Nana al-Bashry? She used to be a friend of my mother's, and yours."

"Really? She preaches now?"

Sayid switches on his blow-dryer at this point and all sound is sucked up in the ensuing roar. My curiosity is piqued.

This Nahed, or Nana, as everyone called her, is someone of my mother's generation whom I have known all my life. Her father was a prominent physician, her mother from a wealthy, landowning family. She completed her studies at the American College for Girls and promptly got married, an arranged marriage, like other girls of her generation and milieu. Nana had intellectual ambitions, however, and fought to get a college degree as a married woman, much against the wishes of her husband, who once burned her notes on the night of a final exam. When their only daughter had an accident that left her severely and permanently retarded, they divorced.

She then tried to make a new start in life. Leaving her child in the care of her mother, she went to England to study for a Ph.D. Brought up in a practicing Muslim environment, I suspect she was a closet agnostic. But in the dreary northern England town where she studied, she had the first of her epiphanies. An Anglophile by education and inclination, the bite of reality in living there as a foreigner compared unfavorably to the ease of her life back home, and the loneliness and prejudice she experienced, or perceived, came as major disillusionments. She never completed her degree.

She came back to Egypt to find her disturbed child—now in a nursing home since her aging mother could no longer cope with the girl—more disturbed than ever. Modern medicine could do nothing to help. Nahed came to perceive the child, and her own failure abroad, as God's will, her burden to bear. She took her daughter back home to her spacious, pleasant villa and shut herself up with her there. And that's when I lost track of her.

"So now she preaches?" I ask Hala, as soon as Sayid switches off the dryer.

"Oh yes, she's very well known. She's studied a great deal, and she's written several books herself, on Islam. She publishes them at her own expense and they're distributed free. But she won't give interviews or go on television or anything like that. Do you know Sheikh Zaki al-Yamani himself asked to meet her and offered to fly her to Saudi Arabia in his private jet if she would lecture over there? But she refused."

"Where does she preach?"

"Well, at the beginning at her own house, she's a bit of a recluse, you know; but more recently she's been giving sermons at a *zawiya* in Mohandesseen, because so many women wanted to attend."

"A zawiya? What, like a Sufi shrine?"

"No, no, nothing to do with that. It's what a small space set aside for prayer is called in Egypt these days. They're usually like a large hall on the ground floor of a building. Many new buildings, in particular, have them, on account of tax deduction incentives."

"Do you think I could attend one of those zawiya meetings?"

Camelia turns around and draws the scarf off her head. "Since when? It's not like you, Nadia."

"No, I think it would be interesting, really."

"Well, we could try. I mean, if we hear there will be a meeting. Because it's usually by word of mouth, you know, that kind of thing," Hala adds dubiously.

Sayid tips my head forward and brushes my hair upside down, then motions me to flip it back. He rub some styling gel in his hands and smoothes my hair. He holds the mirror to the back of my head. "Hair spray? No? There, you're done."

Hala offers to drop me off but I am staying only a few blocks away and I want to pass by the bookshop, Everyman's, that hasn't changed since I was a schoolgirl stopping on my way home to buy Chiclets gum and *Salut les Copains* teen magazines. Despite the "bookshop" sign, Everyman's stocks no books and never has, but you can find most foreign-language magazines, both imported and domestic, along with stationery and small gifts. I pick up the two latest English-language glossies published in Beirut for the Egyptian market: *Cleo* and *Insight.*

Out in the street, there is a hint of *khamaseen* desert wind in the air, and on impulse I remember that I have a scarf to protect my freshly washed hair against the dust. I drape it over my head and loop the ends around my neck and knot them at the back, Audrey Hepburn–style. I try to negotiate the narrow sidewalks of Zamalek, obstructed by parked cars and small cigarette or flower kiosks, and then give up and take to the street.

I am still a couple of blocks from home when I start to feel hot and prickly under the scarf, and slip it off. Almost immediately one taxi after another stops for me, unbidden. "Taxi, Madame?" "Madame, taxi?" It's only then that I realize that no taxi driver had spontaneously offered me a ride while I had walked with my scarf on. Had they made a judgement on my belonging to the walking as opposed to the riding classes based on the scarf?

I get home and make myself a cup of tea, looking forward to settling down with the magazines. Page after page of glossy advertisements for everything from French perfume to Cairo restaurants; a fashion layout featuring Egyptian models in outlandish clothes; and page after "society" page of philanthropic galas and weddings. The women are all dressed and coiffed in the latest fashions, only the rare hijab anywhere in sight. Among the younger set, there is even the occasional exposed midriff or belly button. A complete stranger to Egypt might get the general impression that the women are drawn from a different gene pool than the men, but it is only an illusion created by hair-colorists, makeup artists, and plastic surgeons.

I find the annual list of the Who's Who in Cairo particularly instructive as a reflection of the zeitgeist. Most of the names are unfamiliar, helpfully identified by affiliation to a foreign concession: "Mr. Americana"; "the director of Mobinil and his charming wife"; "Mr. Peugeot." Here and there the names of the heirs or in-laws of former and current presidents pop up—Nasser, Sadat, Mubarak—and of course the ubiquitous Sawiris, Coptic billionaires.

Flipping through the glossy images of conspicuous consumption and over-the-top outfits barely appropriate for Cannes, let alone Cairo, I begin to discern an unarticulated rationale behind Camelia's experimentation with the scarf in front of the mirror.

ॐॐ "They probably just thought you're a foreigner, your hair is so light," suggests Hala when I tell her about my little experience with the headscarf and the taxis on the way home from the hairdresser. It is a week later and I am having Ramadan *iftar* at Hala's, breaking the fast at sunset. "By the way, do you still want to attend one of Doctora Nahed's lectures? She is giving a lecture after sunset prayers in a zawiya in Mohandesseen later this evening."

"Are you going?"

"I try to attend whenever I can squeeze it in between iftar receptions and *sohour* invitations." Hala serves me some Circassian chicken. "Seems like everybody feels they have to entertain during Ramadan, it's becoming very hectic."

"I noticed. Ramadan wasn't that frantically sociable while we were growing up, was it? But then we didn't go to prayers in zawiyas either. In fact I don't ever remember going to a mosque to pray, do you? Do you think we can go this evening?"

"If you like, sure."

"But Mummy," Hala's ten-year-old interrupts, hopping up and down in front of her mother, "you promised to help me with my homework. You have to listen to me recite the poem, and give me the dictation, and . . . "

"It's all right, Sara dear, I'll talk you through it over the phone on my way over there. You can recite the poem to me over the phone. Once you get started you'll be fine." Hala hands me a demitasse of Turkish coffee. "Nadia, we might see Camelia at the zawiya, she's the one who rang up today to tell me about Doctora Nahed; she remembered you'd said you wanted to attend one of her lectures. Remind me to ask Camelia if Hazem has any used computers from his company he can donate to the orphanage. The older kids really need to start learning how to use them. Although I don't know how well Hazem's business has been doing lately; they may be hanging onto their equipment longer."

"Let's call Camelia and find out if she's going."

"She'd be there by now, the prayers have started. We'll have to go after the prayers, just in time for the lecture. I can't pray anyway, I have my period, so it doesn't matter to me. Do you mind?"

"Not at all. Can't we call Camelia on her cell phone? She's sure to have it with her." Everyone in Cairo seems to have a cell phone glued to their ears at all times.

"Yes, but no one would be thoughtless enough to leave it on, not in a place of prayer." Hala makes a reproving face at me as she sips her coffee. We will both have cause to rue that remark.

We finish our coffee and leave. The traffic lull that accompanies iftar has dissipated and driving to Mohandesseen from Dokki takes longer than we expect. One hand on the wheel, one holding the cell phone to her ear, Hala keeps up a three-way conversation with her daughter and me, talking Sara through her homework. Finally we arrive. Hala expertly maneuvers the car into an improvised parking spot on the sidewalk between a cigarette kiosk and a motorcycle, wraps up the conversation with her daughter, and shoves the phone into her voluminous handbag.

The "zawiya" turns out to be a large room on the ground floor of a new apartment building. At the door we stop to take off our shoes. I scan the array of hastily discarded footwear: mostly designer shoes, and some thick-soled basketball shoes of the type fashionable with the teen set. Inside, the eighty or so women and girls are standing around on the prayer mats, chatting. We have timed our arrival just right, after the prayers but before the sermon.

All the women are wearing filmy prayer veils or some type of scarf over their hair, and some have slipped long robes over their street clothes to cover too-short skirts. Both Hala and I conveniently happen to be wearing pantsuits. I knot my silk Hermès scarf under my chin and Hala does the same with a turquoise-colored chiffon that turns her chubby face positively cherubic.

We catch sight of Camelia looking exotic and fetching in a sheer black robe over her clothes and a gold-embroidered headscarf. She waves and we greet each other but she is at the other end of the room. Her daughter is beside her, a petite, quiet girl with a short, simple hairstyle, somewhat in her mother's shadow, it seems to me.

"I think Dina's future in-laws are dragging their feet about doing their part to set up the young couple, from hints I've been picking up," Hala whispers. "Camelia's thinking of giving them an ultimatum or breaking off the engagement."

"Is Dina fond of the boy?"

"That's just the point, she is. I think Camelia's worried that if she lets things go on too long the girl might get too attached to him and then it would be a problem if she had to break it off."

Some things haven't changed, I find myself thinking. So much about Cairo has changed, including the expansion into the new megasuburbs to the east and west, agglomerations of gated compounds with vaguely Americanized names like Green Heights and Palm City, and yet the basic realities of life have not: young couples cannot afford to make their own start in life, and marriage remains an alliance between families and a concerted effort by both sets of parents to set them up as a new atom in the microcosm of their particular social set.

I relax into the busy hum of the women around me, and find myself thinking that the zawiya, in my day, had been the coiffeur: Sayid's salon. That had been our women's space, our weekly ritual.

Just then there is a murmur and a slightly stooped woman in dun-hued, full Islamic dress comes in a side door.

We all settle down and find a spot on the mats, tucking our folded legs under us. The handful of chairs in the back of the room are reserved for the oldest and most arthritic.

Doctora Nahed steps up to the low podium and sits stiff-backed in the chair. She is thinner, older, and smaller than I would have imagined. Her face is bony and dry, and so are the hands she folds on the lectern. I don't recognize her behind the stern spectacles.

When the room is quiet she begins to speak, in a mixture of colloquial and formal Arabic. Her voice, too, is unfamiliar, and I realize that most of the conversations I remember having with Nana El-Bashry were in English. The thrust of her homily is the omnipresent shadow of mortality, and I wonder where she is going with it until I realize it is a call to turn away from the frivolities of the material world. It is a message clearly adapted to her overwhelmingly affluent and worldly audience this evening.

The hardwood floor under the mats is unforgiving and we are all shifting on our haunches. I close my eyes and an image comes unbidden, whole, unexpected, like a gift out of season. Nana El-Bashry, in her late thirties, wearing a bright summer dress with ruffles around the knees, crossing her shapely legs as she sat. I open my eyes and look up to see the bespectacled woman take a break and sip a glass of water.

Hala is whispering in my ear. "My back is killing me, I'm going to go lean against that pillar over there." I nod and she takes advantage of the pause to move unobtrusively over to the pillar. I notice she has left her big handbag behind.

Doctora Nahed starts up again, this time on a different tack. I sit up and take notice when I realize she is actually criticizing one of the most popular preachers on television.

"So when Sheikh Sharmawi said on television, in response to a question, that a woman needs her husband's permission to give charity, a doubt arose in my mind. Then I remembered the story of Aisha and the goat. Now Aisha, the Prophet's wife, had had a goat slaughtered in his absence, and distributed some of the meat to the poor and needy. But more and more people came, and they were equally poor and needy, so she distributed more of the meat. By the time the Prophet, peace be upon him, came home that evening, all she had left to serve him was the neck of the goat."

Tweet . . . tweet. A cell phone's tinny ring breaks the spell. I look around and suddenly realize with horror that it is coming from Hala's bag and that everyone is looking at me accusingly. *Tweet . . . Tweet.* I start to reach for the bag but the ringing stops and I settle down again. How could Hala have forgotten to turn off her cell phone? What if it starts ringing again? I tense up.

Doctora Nahed picks up the thread of her story. "'O messenger of God,' Aisha addressed him. 'I fear that all the goat is gone, and nothing but the neck remains.' 'Aisha,' he is said to have replied, 'it is the other way around. All the goat remains—in God's reckoning, that is—and only the neck is gone.' So what do we learn from this story of Aisha and the goat?"

Suddenly I understand the thrust of her argument. I think I recognize in her the headstrong, independent-minded Nana El-Bishry who rebelled against society's expectations for a woman of her generation; the one who insisted on a divorce, defied convention, and traveled to England with such high hopes of making a new life for herself. She may have come back defeated, but if she submitted to God's plan for her it was on her own terms. And if that means taking on the establishment clerics, she clearly relishes the challenge.

After the lecture I will go over and introduce myself. I am sure she will remember me. Perhaps I can talk to her later, privately. Somehow, if I can recognize the old Nana El-Bashry in this Doctora Nahed, the pieces of a puzzle would fall into place for me.

Tweet . . . tweet. Oh no! I lunge for the bag and plunge my arm into it elbow deep, fumbling around blindly in the jumble of pocketbook and keys, makeup clutch and nail kit. *Tweet . . . tweet.* Kleenex tissues and address book, pens and—ah, finally, the phone. Still ringing shrilly, improbably. *Tweet . . . tweet.* Who keeps ringing on a cell phone for so long? Sara, that's who. Sara who must want her Mummy to attend to her, right this minute, no doubt on a homework-related question. *Tweet . . . tweet.*

Doctora Nahed has fallen silent, reprovingly. Everyone is looking at me. I can hear Camelia trying to apologize on my behalf. "She lives abroad, she doesn't know any better, she didn't think to turn off her phone."

"It's not my phone," I hiss. But I am so flustered I can't find the off switch. *Tweet . . . tweet.*

I look up desperately at Hala and see her crawling toward me on all fours, her rump in the air, her round face uncharacteristically grim in the jolly turquoise scarf. By not standing up, she is trying to avoid attracting attention to herself, but the sight is so comical that I cannot concentrate on finding the off button. I am trying too hard not to laugh out loud. *Tweet . . . tweet.* Hala finally reaches me and grabs the phone. Silence.

Doctora Nahed wraps up her lecture, but I am too dis-combobulated to pay attention. As soon as it is over, I will signal Hala to leave. The embarrassing incident with the cell phone has the effect of operating in me an inexplicable shift in mood; what seemed a bridgeable distance a few minutes ago now seems hopeless. I won't try to speak to Doctora Nahed; even if she remembers me, it is too late now.

The Red Sea

"On your own?" Everyone from my brother to my cousin Hala objects when I tell them that I have suddenly taken it into my mind to spend a week at a Red Sea resort over the Christmas holiday. I am met with reproving glances. "On your own? Why don't you wait till the midyear holidays in January, so you can come with us on vacation? We'll go to the Red Sea if you want." Egyptians never do anything on their own, let alone go on vacation, and such antisocial behavior shocks them. But I insist. Cairo can be overwhelming after a while, and I need a break.

So I am on my own when I check into my second-floor hotel room in Hurghada, on the mainland Egyptian coast of the Red Sea. I immediately go out on the balcony. Wide terraces curve around the hotel's three interlacing pools, cascading down to the deserted beach and the sea. The sun is setting and the horizon is mauve and gold.

"What color is the Red Sea?" people ask me back in North Carolina. I tell them that it is blue; it is the cliffs around it that are sienna red. They ask if you can float in it; no, I answer, that is the Dead Sea, in Jordan.

Far in the distance to my right I can see a rider on a black Arabian, galloping on the beach just beyond the hotel's markers. Even at that distance I can tell that the rider cannot be a paying guest; he must be one of the Bedouin who rent out the horses. He has that loose silhouette, that effortless seat, as if he were gliding on air, barely touching the saddle or the rein. He is riding the horse hard, as if they both need to get the day behind them. Then suddenly he wheels toward the waves and plunges in. The horse paddles, head above water; then the rider floats off and swims out to sea, while the horse heads back for shore. The black horse plods out of the water in the heavy wet sand, momentarily bereft of his grace. He shudders once and then stands still, waiting for his master.

For the first time in fifteen years, for the first time since my accident, I feel the desire to go riding again.

It is ten o'clock when I walk down to the beach the next morning, and most of the deck chairs are already occupied. It is brilliantly sunny, around eighty degrees, desert dry. Vivid red and yellow windsurfer sails dot the striated blues of the water. There is a lively breeze blowing, a little too cool to be lounging around in a swimsuit. The Germans all around me are made of sterner stuff; most of the women are sunbathing topless.

The Swiss Village, where I am staying, is a Swiss-run resort along a private beach a few kilometers from Hurghada proper. The average tourist who comes to Hurghada or Sharm-el-Sheikh bypasses Cairo; on tourist brochures, the vacation is advertised as "Red Sea," no mention of Egypt anywhere. Some tourists think they are in Israel, especially at Sharm-el-Sheikh, in the Sinai.

In Hurghada over the Christmas/New Year holidays, you hear German or Italian or French. Egyptians come at a different time of year, their calendar rhythm is different; it follows the academic year and Muslim holidays. At this winter holiday time of year, there are no Egyptians, and at any time of year, there are no Americans; I am both. At the Swiss Village, the signs all over the hotel are in German, the prices for renting diving equipment are in Euros, and the Egyptian staff speaks German.

When I motion to one of the waiters circulating with trays of frozen strawberry Daiquiris, he speaks to me in German. I don't bother to correct his impression. Today, out here on the beach, in my swimsuit, it's easier to take advantage of the freedom that the provisional status of tourist confers: you shed your skin as you shed your clothes. The French express it so well, that the skin is one more garment like any other: one can be comfortable in one's skin, or not. I am comfortable in my skin, only I have more than one, and sometimes I try them on one at a time, feeling for the best fit. Here at the Red Sea, geographically in Egypt but culturally in a tourist no-man's-land, the choice is not easy.

I stretch out on my long deck chair. The sunbathers are at various stages of "doneness," the new arrivals pale and pasty, the guests nearing the end of their stay baked a deep caramel color. For no reason, I find myself wondering what my grandmother would make of the tan, sculpted ideal of beauty today, Nanou for whom seduction in a woman started with being soft and white; who would say, when she saw a woman with muscular arms, "She has arms like a washerwoman."

Stupefied by the sun and the wind off the water, I idly consider the options on the list of suggested activities posted on the flyer in my room. I could go on one of the many diving excursions, or I could rent a jet ski or a windsurfer or a horse. I haven't been riding for years, not since a fall long ago left me with two fused vertebrae and a terminal reluctance to get back in the saddle. That was shortly before I immigrated to the States. I tell myself that vacations are supposed to be a time to try new experiences, or experiences so far in the past they count as new.

A masseur comes by, a Nubian in an orange jersey who looks like a body-builder; he tries to coax guests to come over to his massage table under a palm tree on the beach. He seems particularly persistent with two attractive young German women. Finally one of them laughs and gets up and lies down on her stomach on the towel-covered table. She points to her back and shoulders as she unhooks the top half of her bikini. "Shoulders only," she seems to be saying.

The wind is quite brisk and I pull the towel over me like a sheet. I try to read but the glare reflected off the turquoise water gets in my eyes. A few meters out from shore a half-dozen children are riding a long, caterpillar-shaped, inflatable raft pulled along by a small motorboat. Two Egyptian "animators" from the hotel are giving windsurfing lessons to slightly older children.

A raised voice makes me look up. The woman on the massage table looks annoyed. She raises herself on her elbows. "Half-body only. Shoulders only, understand?" And lies back down. The masseur ignores her.

The woman raises her voice again, exasperated but more amused than upset. She swings her legs off the table and walks off, laughing, her bikini top dangling from her hand. The masseur drops his hands to his sides and looks down, sly and unabashed.

I get up and walk down to the water and test it with my foot: brisk but not daunting. I put on fins and a mask, hold my breath, and plunge in. After the initial numbing sting, the cold water is invigorating. I swim rapidly out to sea to get warm, trying to keep clear of the annoying wake of the caterpillar with its load of squealing children. When I come out of the water the wind against my wet skin is chilling and I dash back to my hotel room. As I towel off in front of the mirror I can already make out the outline of my swimsuit, just a ghost of a shade lighter than the exposed skin. I peel back the covers and jump into the cool white sheets. Bliss. Tomorrow, I think, I will go riding; I repeat the words to myself to test how convincing I sound.

An hour later I dress for dinner: loose silk pants, small silk top, both in moss green; high-heeled sandals. On the way to the dining room I stop at the reception desk to return the hair dryer I have borrowed earlier. The manager comes out from behind his desk with a discreet smile. He has apparently recognized my maiden name and asks me if I am related to "the well-known politician." I acknowledge that I am his niece, wondering if the man realizes that my uncle passed away months ago.

The hotel offers breakfast and dinner buffet style in the main dining room, or à la carte in any of the other restaurants. This evening, since I am on my own, I opt for the buffet in order to feel less self-conscious. The main dining room is already full, and a line has formed in front of the buffet tables. The family waiting in line ahead of me, parents and two white-blond children, all hold their dinner plates at their sides like discus throwers.

The couple behind me are speaking French, and that is unusual enough in itself for me to notice them. She is wearing a filmy blue sundress with a filmy little scarf around the neck; he is wearing a navy sweater slung across his shoulders and knotted in front, over a pink shirt with sleeves rolled up just so.

They are looking around for a free table, and so am I; the maître d'hôtel asks us if we wouldn't mind sharing. We introduce ourselves: they are Julienne and Philippe, from Brussels. When I tell them that I am Egyptian originally, that I grew up in Cairo, they lean forward and ask me in confidential tones if I know where one can go to get an authentic local meal.

"Julienne is dying for a good couscous, aren't you, *ma chérie?*"

Where did they think they were, I wondered. "This isn't Morocco, you know; Egyptians don't eat couscous. Besides, a lot of the dishes on the buffet are authentically Egyptian."

They look unconvinced. "Yes, but we like to eat *chez l'habitant,* with the locals. Where can we get a meal at some authentic bistro?"

"Not here. There's nothing but hotels and beaches for miles and miles. And the locals—well, I don't think they have a cuisine as such."

Julienne looks disappointed; Philippe pats her hand and murmurs, "Don't worry, ma chérie, we'll find you your couscous."

I suggest the land tour by Jeep into the desert, lunch with the Bedouin included, as described in the flyer of activities. I know there will be no couscous, and the lunch, I suspect, will have been prepared by the hotel, but the tour guides are adept at satisfying fantasies of authenticity.

We part on the friendliest of terms and they head for the pool table on the second floor while I head back to my room.

I stretch out on the bed and switch on the satellite television. There are three German channels, two Italian, one French, one British, one Gulf Arab, and one Egyptian, reflecting, I suppose, the hotel's clientele. I switch from a highly explicit film on the French channel to a turbaned Islamic scholar reciting from the Koran on another; it's a bit of a jolt.

᭞᭞It is mid-afternoon again and I am on the deck of the glass-bottom boat, a few miles out to sea, when the captain points to the distance. A school of dolphins flash in and out of the water, like a benediction. Then we head back in the direction of the hotel marina and we have a wide-angle view of the coastline: the narrow strip of beach with its string of bright hotels, the stretches of no-man's-land in between, and beyond, the low mountains looming sienna red and barren.

In the distance I see the black horse again, cantering. This time I can see the rider better: he is wearing an Arab headdress and a galabiya hiked up over jeans. He reins in the horse and they are silhouetted against the cloudless sky. Then he raises his hand to his ear; he is talking into a cellular phone. I wish I had my camera; it's the sort of incongruous image that I find worth capturing.

Today, I tell myself, I will go riding at sunset. I make it a pledge, a dare. This time, I believe in it; I can tell because a knot of apprehension is forming in my stomach.

᭞᭞I walk down to where the four or five horses are tethered just outside the perimeter of the hotel. The three grooms look like they're ready to call it a day. I recognize the black horse.

"What's his name?" I ask, in Arabic.

"That's the owner's, no one else rides him. But you can take your pick of these three. Do you ride?"

I shake my head.

"Then one of us will have to go with you, and that's double the price. Well, let's saddle up Sakran for you." He starts to untether a chocolate brown gelding.

"Sakran? Drunkard? That's not very reassuring!"

"We just call him that because he drinks a lot. Not to worry, he's not mean."

The owner comes up, still wearing the headdress but no galabiya, just the jeans and a shirt. He is younger than I expected and lighter-complexioned than the typical Upper Egyptian. He says something sharply to the groom about tightening the girth; the horse is inflating his stomach with air and the saddle will be dangerously loose when he deflates.

"*Yallah*, come on, lady." He bends over slightly and cups his hands for me to place my knee in them. I shake my head and ask him to bring the horse around to the watering trough so I can stand on it and climb onto the saddle on my own. He frowns a little, puzzled, trying to decide if it is prudishness on my part. But I know, from experience, that I don't have the upper body strength to hoist myself, even with a leg up; he would end up having to lift me bodily into the saddle, an indignity I would rather avoid. The man shrugs and leads the horse around to the trough. When I am astride he checks the length of the stirrups.

"Keep your heels down. If you don't your whole foot will go through the stirrup in these running shoes. Then if you happen to fall off . . . "

"The horse will drag me. I know."

"Okay. Mohamed here will go with you."

Mohamed takes the mean-eyed chestnut mare and we set off on the wet sand at the water's edge. Mohamed is wearing worn gym shoes, his feet dangling out of the stirrups, but I know it doesn't matter what he wears; these grooms are all the same, they can ride barefoot or bareback with the same insolent ease.

The sun is setting, and I look out to sea, bathing my eyes in the gray-blue gleam of the water. Sakran starts trotting although I am not spurring him and I realize Mohamed is making hissing-clicking sounds to get him going.

"Don't," I warn. "I'm just enjoying this pace for now."

But I don't get to enjoy it for long. Mohamed is both impatient and talkative. He keeps asking me questions about where I'm from, where I live, what family I have. I've established that I'm Egyptian but he can tell there is something different about me, if only because I am alone. He asks me what I do; I pretend not to hear. When he gets nowhere with this line of questioning he tries to coax me to break into a gallop.

"Yallah, let's go," he clicks and hisses at the horse, and I am annoyed at being at the mercy of his remote control; he could at least grant me the illusion of being in charge of my own mount. Now he goes on about how bad business is.

"So you all do most of your business at this time of year then? And I suppose Egyptians only come during the mid-year vacation and in summer?"

"Let the Egyptians stay home," he says bitterly. "Who needs them! Now your khawaga, your tourist, if he spends a lot of time with you, when he goes he leaves you a pair of used gym shoes, or one of those disposable cameras, or a watch."

Mohamed's constant whining, all angling at a big tip, is spoiling the sunset and the ride for me. "Let's go back." I turn Sakran around.

"But you still have half an hour to go."

"That's all right, I'm tired."

When we get back to the stable I tip him, nevertheless, out of habit.

"Come back tomorrow," the grooms smile at me. "Come take a trek to the mountains with us."

"*Inshallah*," I reply, noncommittal. This abortive excursion by remote control has not conquered my memories, good or bad. It's as if trying to ride again is a rite of passage in relearning how to live in Egypt. If I can get behind the wheel to brave Cairo traffic, I tell myself, I can overcome my fear of getting back in the saddle. I have to try again.

సౌసౌTomorrow is Christmas Eve. I have forgotten, in spite of the big cardboard sleigh full of empty, wrapped boxes decorating the lobby, and *White Christmas* blaring from the discotheque by the pool. All the animators are going around the pool and the beach, getting the guests signed up for the Christmas Eve "gala" at the hotel. I am lying on my deck chair, reading, when one of them blows a noisemaker in my ear. I look up to see a heavyset Egyptian wearing a ridiculous Santa hat trying to "jolly me up" in German. I fix the man with my most unamused look and answer in Arabic, which disconcerts him. He apologizes and I feel a twinge of embarrassment for him; Egyptians are temperamentally ill-suited to this artificial bonhomie.

Around noon I get up to go back to my room. As I wind my way around the deck chairs straddled by men in Speedos and women in thongs, I suddenly glimpse a group of three elderly Egyptian women wearing silk scarves knotted under the chin, long-sleeved shirts, and trousers with shoes. What are Egyptians doing here at this time of year? They wouldn't be staying at the hotel proper, they must be staying in one of the private time-share units adjacent to the hotel, where Egyptians families prefer to stay. But this is the wrong time of year. Elderly women, obviously respectable and middle-class; they must be too old to be tied down to the academic and work schedules of children and husbands, and free to get away for a few days for a little fresh air and rest.

The three women are chatting together quietly, seemingly oblivious to the nudity around them. I wonder if they feel out of place, or if, on the other hand, the sight of these covered-up women makes the near-naked tourists uncomfortable. Perhaps I am the only one who is uncomfortable.

෧෧Christmas Eve. The festivities take place under a huge tent adjacent to the pool. A raised dais at one end is reserved for the band and the floor show. Each table is crowned with a champagne bottle in an ice bucket and laden with bags of party favors. I am on my own but the Belgian couple spot me immediately and wave me over to their table. They never did find their couscous but they hooked up with some other tourists and rented a taxi for an overnight trip to Luxor and are exhausted but thrilled with their excursion. The Germans all around us are pelting each other, the waiters, and total strangers at other tables with the little hard papier-mâché balls you find in the bags of party favors.

Perhaps they are bored with the less than riveting floor show; it consists of cabaret, Nubian, Russian, and oriental dancing, all seemingly provided by the same inexhaustible troupe of skinny blondes, probably Russian, and voluptuous brunettes, of indeterminate nationality. I know for a fact that they are not Egyptian, whatever they are, the minute they try to belly dance. When they come out, resplendent in sequined bikinis and colorful veils, tossing their long hair and jiggling their breasts, I start to laugh until I realize that it is not meant to be a parody. I am thinking that it's lucky for them I am the only Egyptian in the audience, when I look around and glimpse the three elderly women in head-scarves at a table at the far end, clapping obligingly at the urging of the animators.

I am trying to decide whether it is worth sitting it out till midnight, when the whirling dervish comes on. He leaps onto the stage, a spiral of uncoiled energy, already twirl-ing to a primal drumbeat and a hypnotic chant of *"nadart, nadart,"* two cones of bright fabric revolving and dissolving as he steps into and out of his skirt and cape, always whirling, never hesitating, unwinding his turban and letting his long black bangs whip around his absent eyes. "Nadart, nadart," I have pledged, I have pledged, still whirling—the audience is on its feet now—he lies down on his side and one arm goes on twirling the cape over his head, "nadart, nadart," he jumps up and forges into the gasping audience, twirling the cape over their heads, and close up you see the sweat beading on his smooth face; he is hardly more than a boy with an ath-lete's insolence, twirling, always whirling, he climbs back on the stage and drops into a split on the floor and glares directly at the audience for the first time as the drumbeat comes to a stop with a savage clap: "nadart, nadart, ya rasul allah." I have pledged, I have pledged, O messenger of God.

There is a moment's hush, then enthusiastic applause, as the dervish and the chanting drummers exit. But a whiff of something disturbing and unseemly, like sweat, lingers in the air. The tourists seem vaguely uneasy and momentarily hushed. I can imagine them thinking: these Egyptians are the same people, after all, the wild dervishes, and these suave waiters who serve us while we lie topless on the beach; that is what they are really like then, these people, that savage drumbeat is in their blood. The tourists must be wondering how safe they are, even here at the Red Sea.

&&Sunset. I head down to the horses. This time the owner saddles Sakran for me himself. "Listen," he suggests as he makes me stand in the stirrups and then adjusts them down a notch. "The grooms tell me you can ride a little. Why don't you go on your own? You'll be all right. Just remember to keep your heels down."

I wonder if he guesses that I was put off by Mohamed's endless patter or whether Mohamed himself was dissatisfied with my largesse. All things considered, I decide to take my chances alone with the Drunkard. I ignore the knot of apprehension in my stomach.

I set off at a leisurely pace, looking out to sea at the hot pink and blood orange horizon reflected in the deepening blue of the water. Sakran plods along, getting his hooves wet, avoiding the occasional rock or rusty can on the no-man's stretch of beachfront between the hotels. As the sun sinks, I spur him into a trot, then a canter, then a gallop when we are on an upward incline or where the sand is deep and dry enough to discourage him from taking it into his head to make a break for the stable. I am exhilarated. Tomorrow, I think, I will take him all out.

Suddenly Sakran comes to a dead stop and I am slammed forward onto his neck, nearly losing my seat. I clutch at his neck and try to find the stirrups with my feet, heart pounding. Then I see what spooks him. Hang gliders jumping off from the russet cliffs are landing on the beach in front of us, the brilliant parachutes ballooning, then swaying as they hit the ground, like giant drunken birds. Sakran stands rock still, quivering, his ears straining forward.

"It's all right." I stroke his neck. "It's all right." I try to nudge him forward, but he quivers again and tosses his head and I duck to avoid a blow to the chin.

"All right, Sakran, let's go back then, come on boy." I try to wheel him around but he ignores me. I consider getting off and leading him back on foot. Then I sigh and sit back in the saddle. We can just wait it out, Sakran and I. Just stay still for as long as it takes. I don't know whether he will move forward or turn back when he comes out of his trance. All I can do is stroke him and murmur reassuringly. And remember to keep my heels down, in case he decides to bolt.

The Mango Orchard

It was the second day of the Lesser Feast that marks the end of Ramadan, and I was having dinner at my brother Omar's; the only other guests were Hala and her husband. My sister-in-law Layla apologized that Omar was late, but would join us as soon as he could. He was on his way back from the country, where he'd been called unexpectedly early that morning. A murder had taken place in a mango orchard Omar and I inherited from Nanou, on the outskirts of a small village.

"I don't have any other details, but I'm sure Omar will tell us all about it when he gets here. But he insisted we don't hold up dinner." Layla led the way to the dining room. "Let's go ahead, please, I insist."

I was intrigued. My brother and I had inherited the orchard from Nanou a few years ago. When Nanou was alive, she sent all her children crates of sweet Alphonse mangoes every season, and sold the rest of the crop for a handsome profit. But after her death we saw precious few mangoes from the orchard, and fewer every year. The entire village was under the thumb of a local bully, the *baltagui*; the orchard keeper shared the crop with him. Once a year the keeper brought a few crates of mangoes, as a sop, to Omar's villa in Zamalek, with loud lamentations of how poor the crop had been, how this bug or that had decimated it.

Finally Omar had enough, hired two watchmen with rifles, and sent them to guard the orchard when the mangoes started to ripen. The baltagui and some of his henchmen gathered at night and strung the watchmen up in the trees, with a warning that if they set foot in the orchard again they would be strung up dead. The next morning when they were discovered and cut down, the watchmen ran away and Omar could find no one to replace them. He tried to find a buyer for the orchard to get it off his hands, but whenever a buyer came he was driven off by the baltagui. So the mango orchard now languished from neglect, and even the little barefoot boys did not dare help themselves to the fruit that fell and rotted on the ground.

We were halfway through dinner when Omar came in, looking tired and dusty; he is an architect, with little time or aptitude for agricultural pursuits.

"Sorry I'm late! Just give me a minute to wash up and I'll tell you all about it," he promised. In a few minutes he joined us at the table and told us the story between sips of soup.

That morning, the second day of the Feast, he had received a phone call out of the blue: a murder had been committed in our mango orchard. Omar drove up to the country right away and met with the village policeman in charge of the case, a young man with a black moustache cutting a neat slash across his narrow bronze face.

Ahmed the policeman said he knew right away, when he offered his condolences to the father of the victim and was met with "Who says my son is dead?"

The father glared at the policeman, his paunchy bulk in a brown galabiya barring the rickety wooden door. "Who says my son is dead? My son is not dead—yet."

The baltagui said this, "eyeball to eyeball" as the police-man related, despite the fact that he—Ahmed—could glimpse the toes of the corpse as it lay covered with a sheet on the long table in the main room of the single-story house. Despite the fact that the body lay there, unburied, in violation of Islamic custom, although the call for midday prayers had come and gone. Despite the fact that in the heat of the Egyptian countryside, the body would start to stink within hours. Which meant that the father would have to act quickly. That's when the policeman knew what he had to do. If he did nothing, the killer would come to him—but it might already be too late.

The policeman walked away from the house where a dead body lay and no women wailed. He started to head back slowly along the dusty unpaved street, adjusting his cap to wipe the perspiration from his brow. "Allah forgive us," he muttered, "and on the day of the Feast." Who had a blood grudge against the victim? Almost anyone in the village had a grievance against his father the baltagui, the village bully. But they feared him even more than they hated him. The villagers must know who killed the baltagui's son; this was a small vil-lage, after all, and the killing occurred in broad daylight.

But Ahmed the policeman was not really one of them. He was from an identical village in the same province of the northeast, and only a generation better educated than most of them, but he was an outsider. Ahmed had been assigned to the district that included this village called Mit Halfa—One Hundred Oaths—four months ago; it was only his sec-ond assignment.

Ahmed wondered who of the baltagui's many enemies would want to assassinate his son. But why the son and not the father? To intimidate him? That made as much sense as killing a lion cub and letting the lioness loose. Ahmed walked on, weighing various possibilities in his mind. He had been warned about the bully when he was assigned, and he had known that one day he would have to confront the man. Now it looked as if the moment had come.

Ahmed the policeman made his way along the dusty alleys of the village, taking his time, his eyes and ears alert to pick up a sign. He was in no hurry. The killer would come to him. He only had to make himself available. He greeted the men sitting on a bench by their door stoops smoking or sipping small glasses of tea. They returned his greeting soberly and did not offer him a sip of tea, which would have been an invitation to talk. Most of the doors to the mud-brick houses were closed, and here and there a woman drew a wooden window shutter.

Even the children tracing lines in the dust with little toy wheels at the end of a stick seemed subdued. There was no school today, it being the first day of the Lesser Feast. Otherwise around this time of day the children would have been filing home from the one-room whitewashed mosque, carrying their school books in plastic bags, the girls solemn in head scarves, the cheeky boys cropped-headed. The bakery and the few other shops were also closed for the Feast. The pack of dogs sniffed around the trash heap. A few brightly colored streamers and Ramadan paper lanterns hung, tattered, from the trees.

There was an unnatural stillness in the air, a heaviness of waiting, like a big-bellied woman with child. When a tree rustled, when a water buffalo bellowed in the clover field, when a flatbed truck rattled past on the paved road half a mile away, every living creature seemed to hold its breath and listen. Listen for what, waiting for what? Ahmed knew. Waiting for someone to die. But perhaps he could still prevent it, if the killer came to him. He turned around and started back down the one-street village at a measured pace.

The call for late afternoon prayers soared, amplified, from the minaret of the one-room mosque. "The afternoon; and Man is lost." The verses from the Koran went through his head, idly. Ahmed sighed and muttered "God forgive us" under his breath, thinking of the unburied body on the long table. Today, the first day of the Lesser Feast that marked the end of the long month of fasting, should have been a day of festivities. Yesterday evening, when the radio had announced that the new moon had been officially spotted, there had been a bustle in the village: the voices of women exchanging Feast greetings over the lines of washing strung up between the houses, calling to their children to catch a chicken and wring its neck for the festive dinner; the children squealing as they chased a flapping hen around the yard. The men had lined up at the bakery to stock up on bread for the three days of the Feast. The lines had been unusually long, and the baker even more short-tempered than usual.

Something flickered in the back of the police officer's mind. There had been an altercation at the bakery, some kind of brawl, nothing out of the ordinary; by the time he had been called it had apparently blown over. Who had been involved? He had seen the baker's nephew slumped on the ground, a thin boy of about sixteen, with tears on his long black lashes and blood on his downy upper lip. Someone had given him a brutal beating. Who? The boy had only wiped his nose on his sleeve and shook his head when Ahmed questioned him.

Ahmed turned around and headed along the ditch toward the baker's house. Salim Abdullah the baker and his family lived in two rooms above the bakery. He had four children and an orphan nephew who worked as his helper in the shop. Ahmed knocked on the door, loudly, and waited. He was glad the bakery was closed for the Feast; it must be intolerably hot here when the ovens were blasting away. He peered through the murky window, now closed, through which the baker served his customers. The long, level baking trays were stacked neatly next to the round, shallow rush baskets in which the piles of bread loaves would be carried, the baskets expertly balanced on the head of the women or the little boys on bikes. Some villagers still prepared their bread dough at home and brought the flat disks of dough to the baker to be baked while the children waited outside to carry it home. "Leave the baking to the baker, even if he eats half the bread," the proverb went. Not that this baker was dishonest, only hot-tempered, understandably, slaving away as he did in front of the blazing oven in all seasons. The policeman knocked again, louder.

Someone cracked open a window upstairs and looked down onto the street, then the shutter was yanked shut. Finally he heard the baker clattering down the spiral metal stairs. He came to the door and opened it quickly, part way, darting glances up and down the street. He drew Ahmed in by the arm and closed and bolted the door behind him. "What do you want?" The baker was a tall man in a white cotton galabiya, the sleeves rolled up over his sinewy baker's forearms. An odd mixture of emotions played across his hawk-nosed face: fear, but also relief. "What do you want from me?"

"I only wanted to speak to your nephew for a minute."

"What for? He hasn't done anything."

"I know. I only wanted to ask him about that brawl yesterday evening."

"I'll tell you all you need to know."

The story came out then.

The line had formed in front of the bakery as soon as the radio had announced that the new moon had been sighted. The baker had worked like a man possessed, baking batch after batch of the round flat loaves, leaving his nephew in the front of the store behind the counter window to serve the customers. At first the mood had been festive but as the line lengthened and so did the wait, the men began to grumble, the children jostled. The baker fell further and further behind, and the customers in the back of the line fretted that he would run out of bread and exhorted those up front not to buy more than their share. The nephew had trouble keeping order; the sweat was running down his forehead and into his long-lashed eyes. The baker came to the window and shouted that everyone would be served in turn but that no one was to take more than ten loaves at once. Then he went back inside.

What happened next he learned later. The baltagui's oldest son, Gibali, showed up and elbowed his way to the front of the line. The crowd muttered but parted for him. Everyone knew Gibali; at eighteen he already had his father's paunch and his belligerence. He banged on the counter and demanded to have his basket filled with bread.

The baker's nephew told him he could only have the same amount as everybody else. Gibali yanked him out from behind the counter and beat him savagely, calling him the son of a dog and the son of a whore. Then he scooped the bread off the counter into his basket and stalked off. When the baker came out to see what the commotion was about, he found his nephew crumpled to the ground, a tooth piercing his lower lip. The crowd shook their heads and muttered after Gibali, "His day will come," and "there is no power but God's."

Early the next morning the baker was walking back from the mosque after dawn prayers when he saw the baltagui's son walking in the mango orchard. The baker yelled out to him. Gibali tossed down the mango in his hand and ran. The baker chased him; all that was on his mind at that moment, he swore, was to teach the young bully a lesson. Gibali ran in the direction of the nearest house and banged the door open, shouting for help. The baker followed on his heels. The women in the room cowered in a corner—the men were still at the mosque, exchanging Feast-day greetings. The baker fell upon Gibali and they struggled. The younger man pulled out a knife and the baker turned it against him and stuck it in his throat. Then he let the body drop to the ground and strode off. He was halfway home when the women started screaming. Since then he had locked himself up in the house, waiting for the baltagui to come for him.

"He won't bury his son till he has drunk of my blood."

Ahmed nodded; he had known that from the moment the baltagui had met him with "Who says my son is dead? My son is not dead—yet."

"You should have come to me right away," Ahmed told him. "But thank God it's not too late. Salim Abdullah, I am arresting you for the manslaughter of Gibali Hassanein. Now follow me to the police station. You'll be safe there. You can tell the family you're going, but hurry, it will be sunset soon." Ahmed spoke with a calm that he did not feel; escorting this prisoner from his doorstep to the jailhouse two kilometers away on foot would be the most dangerous thing he had ever done.

They stepped out the door into air thick with the twittering of birds bedding down in the trees; the call for sunset prayers rang out against the chatter. Almost as soon as they set foot in the street the pack of dogs started to follow them like a curse. People turned to watch them pass and heads appeared at doors and windows. The muezzin's call rose and fell, rose and then fell silent, the echo hanging in the air. Ahmed headed straight for the main road; they would be safer on the road with the headlights of trucks passing. Then they would have about a kilometer to walk to the district police station.

The sky had turned a deep pink and night would fall rapidly. Ahmed decided to cut across the mango orchard to reach the road; it was quicker and he would avoid passing in front of the baltagui's house. He lifted the latch of the gate and went into the orchard with the baker, relatching the gate behind them, locking out the pack of dogs. In the orchard it was darker and cooler; the deep irrigation ditches of fine gray-brown soil running between the rows of waxy-leafed mango trees were dry. The two men hurried, stumbling over squishy rotten fruit underfoot. They were halfway through the small orchard when men dropped from the trees and a blow on the head rendered Ahmed unconscious.

&&The sun was coming up behind the clover field and the water buffaloes were lowing when Ahmed drove down the road with a reinforcement of two other policemen. They parked the car where the dirt road narrowed and the ditch began. They continued on foot through the village, and even from that distance they could hear the women wailing. The wailing was coming from the direction of the baker's house—his body had been found in the ditch of the mango orchard and now lay on the long kneading table of the bakery. The morticians were washing the body and wrapping it in a white sheet to ready it for burial before the noon prayers were called. The policemen shook their heads and murmured "God forgive us" and "God have mercy on his soul." The villagers they passed repeated "Amen" and "We are all in God's hands." It was as if the spell of eerie silence had been broken. What they had been waiting for had come to pass.

As Ahmed and his men approached the baltagui's house they heard more wailing coming from that direction. Ahmed heard it with relief; it had made his skin crawl, yesterday, that house where a dead body lay and no women wailed. The three policemen tightened their grips on their guns and knocked. They waited uneasily. Then they knocked again. It was the baltagui himself who suddenly yanked open the door. He stood there, his bulk in his blood-stained brown galabiya blocking the doorway, but Ahmed could see that there was no body on the table: the baltagui had buried his son before the cock crowed.

"Mitwali Hassanein, it is my duty to take you in for questioning in the killing of Salim Abdullah the baker . . ." Ahmed began.

"You can take me in," retorted the baltagui, "but first have the courtesy of offering me condolences on the death of my son. Did no one tell you that my son is dead? I buried him this dawn. Let no one say that I buried my son while his killer drew breath."

Night Journeys

I wonder what people did, before they knew the earth was round, before they realized that it was always daylight somewhere else on earth. How did they ward off the despair of the darkest hours, when they had to take it on faith that day would break?

I can't sleep, and I wish I could call him. It is two o'clock Wednesday morning here in Cairo, but only seven o'clock Tuesday evening for him on the East Coast of the States. All around him the town is still awake and bustling and brightly lit, the day barely winding down, the evening news droning in the background, the phone ringing, dinner plans in the offing. Still the whole evening ahead of him, and then the whole night to get through.

I tell myself it wouldn't do any good to call him; I need to talk to someone who has been through the night already, who has traversed the darkest hours and made it to the other side. Someone who lives closer to where the sun rises, in Japan or Australia, who could reassure me that the new day has broken already. It doesn't work in reverse.

But tonight I have an overwhelming urge to tug on the Ariadne's thread that connects me to him like a lifeline, like a cable under the oceans to the other end of the world. So I send him a discreet message over the cyberthread that links us. Just this: Are you there? If you happen to be sitting before your screen, if you happen to be connected, you will see the little flag go up, and you will recognize my alias; you will reply, and we can have a conversation in real time.

It's so late, I should go to bed, but I wish I could reach you. At any rate I can't sleep again tonight, and I won't even try till the call for dawn prayers has come and gone. I know I will lie tense in bed till I hear it, and even if I did manage to doze off, it would wake me with the heart-pounding shock of a siren going off directly into my ear. These days the call to prayer is blared over loudspeakers, but it wasn't always so. When I was a child, and happened to be awake at dawn, I would hear the muezzin's chant drifting up faint as a plume of smoke in the sky, so musical I sometimes opened my windows to hear it better.

Where you are, it is nowhere near dawn. If you're at the beach house, you will be alone. Are you sitting at your computer? But even if you are sitting in your armchair reading, with your back to the desk, you might hear the little *ping* and turn to the screen. So I leave my missive there, and wait. It takes time, I know, for messages to cross the vast distance between us, even in the ether.

You know, long before cyberspace, there were all these myths, in this part of the world, about enchanted travel across the seas and the continents: the magic carpets of the *Thousand and One Nights,* Sinbad the Sailor hitching a ride on the Roc. And then there is the legend of the original night journey, of the winged horse that flew the Prophet from Mecca to the Furthest Mosque.

If I could, I would ride my message over the ether like a magic carpet. I'd open the balcony window, and kneel down on a small rug, and close my eyes, and find myself lifted up and away. The wind rushes against my face, and I keep my eyes tight shut, because it's a long way down, and that's the secret of magic carpets: you mustn't look down, or the carpet dips and you fall to the ground. It gets chillier and chillier as I fly along, concentrating very hard on homing in on you; there is no other way to steer a magic carpet. It is getting lighter as I fly west, lighter and colder. I lose my concentration for a second and feel the carpet dip and weave, and I clamp down on my thoughts again.

I am getting very tired, and chilled through, and I begin to doubt I can hold on till I reach you. But then I feel the carpet begin to weave downward, and I open my eyes to see the gray Atlantic rushing toward me in the moonlight, the ghostly sand dunes, the long grasses along the path leading up from the beach, the shadow of the shape of a house. Then the carpet whooshes across the deck, through the open French doors, and I jump off as it skims the smooth tiles.

I stand there, catching my breath, and look around. This is the sunroom, with the white wicker furniture and the white linen draperies hanging from polished wood oars in lieu of rods. I wonder why you left the French doors open at night, but then again, I don't. I stand still, listening to the lullaby of the surf, listening for some sound to guide me to the room you're in. I hear a low bark, and Bach pads toward me on his big fluffy paws. He stands in the doorway, then turns and looks over his shoulder, wagging, and I follow him. I hear muted sounds upstairs; you must be in the room with the bookcases, the one with the best view of the ocean. You told me once you had the beach house built with the bedrooms downstairs and the living areas upstairs to make the most of the seascape.

I follow Bach up the stairs and stop at the doorway. You have your back to me; you're in a worn blue bathrobe, looking for a book on the shelves. There is music playing low in the background—Eric Clapton. (A classical concert is more your style, I know, but it's my fantasy, and if I am to steer a magic carpet to the sound of a siren call, it has to at least have the grinding backbeat of "You had one chance / and you blew it." No? All right then, let's compromise, Andrea Bocelli.

You turn around, book in hand, and settle down in the recliner, patting your pockets for your glasses. You don't see me. If only you looked up, I would rush across the room and slither into your lap; I'd sigh and snuggle down, and slip my chilled hands under the lapel of your bathrobe. And you'd laugh and take your glasses off, and shift my weight around, and I'd say, "Am I heavy?"

And you'd answer, "No, just getting comfortable."

And it would be that simple.

But you don't see me. I stand there until you put the book down, and get up and start hunting around the bookcase again. As soon as you turn your back, I'm gone.

You didn't look up, you didn't see the little flag; you didn't hear the *ping.* Or perhaps you're not at the beach house at all. Perhaps you're having dinner out, or you've gone back to the city.

Do you know, in our year together, in our year of living dangerously, so long ago now, I always told you about my dreams, especially dreams about you. They were warning signals, I realize now: I would dream that I was driving along a cliff and a car just like yours was following me, trying to drive me off the road. Or that I heard your voice calling me, and turned around, and it was you, but you looked different somehow: you were clean-shaven, or you were wearing different glasses. When I reported my dreams to you, you'd rub your beard and shoot questions at me like an inquisitor: Did your father wear glasses? Your husband is clean-shaven, isn't he? But it had nothing to do with that, I realize now; my dreams were subliminal warnings that I didn't really know you; I didn't really see you.

But whenever I asked you if you dreamed about me, you'd say no, never, you only had fantasies. I didn't know, at the time, how much you dreaded betraying any loss of control. Because fantasies are something you control, aren't they, and dreams take you over.

But it is too late now for understanding to do any good, and too late for misunderstanding also.

I should turn off the screen and get into bed, but I don't feel sleepy and I keep wondering where you are. I think of a poem by a brilliant Arab poet, called El-Mutanabi, the Pretender, for his arrogance. It begins "O daughter of Time, I have all Time's daughters / How did you reach me through the throng?"

The daughters of Time were misfortunes, and this particular poem was about a mysterious night visitor who comes to haunt him in his bed; he never knows when she will make an appearance, so he spreads pillows and cushions for her, but when she comes, she refuses to lie anywhere but between his ribs. It sounds erotic, but it turns out he was writing about a recurrent fever. Tonight I hope you're tossing and turning in your bed, wherever you are; I wish I could come to haunt you, and burrow into your ribs, and worry you till you ache.

That Which Does Not Kill Us

For five years in the mid-nineties, there were four of us who formed the regular Monday-Wednesday walking group in Duke Forest: Martine, Janice, Penny, and me. Come rain, shine, or high water over the creek, we set off at eight o'clock in the morning for our four-mile loop twice a week. By the time we dispersed, five years later, one of us had achieved a secret ambition; the husband of one had triumphed in a corporate rivalry over the husband of the other; and one of us had experienced a tragedy none of us could have imagined in our darkest moments.

I hadn't thought of the walking group in a while, until an article in today's local paper—about four Duke students on the lacrosse team who are accused of raping a young stripper at a rowdy party in an off-campus house—suddenly pulled those memories into focus, like a blurred photo you decipher for the first time.

The loop we four women took at Duke Forest on our walks back then entailed certain risks, but rape was hardly on the list. The greatest challenge was crossing the bridge over the creek, often flooded when it had rained heavily. Going back the way we came was not an option; it would have added an hour to the walk. The first thing to do was to test the depth of the water by throwing a stone into it. If the stone made a shallow splash, we tiptoed across in our hiking shoes, splat, splat. If the water was too deep, there was no help for it; we took off our socks and shoes and sloshed right into it barefoot. In summer, when we wore shorts and the water was warm, it was not unpleasant, except for the bits of gravel that invariably stuck to the soles of our feet when we put our socks and shoes back on. In cold weather we took off our shoes and rolled up our pant legs and hopped across the bridge as fast as we could. Our feet stayed chill and damp in our soggy socks for the rest of the long walk. Janice's Charlie, who was mostly cocker spaniel, crossed the bridge with us or swam across the creek; but Penny's Lizzie, an indecipherable mix, was afraid of water and had to be carried.

One time in early spring when we found the creek flooding over the bridge, we sat down on logs nearby and took off our shoes and socks and started to roll up our pants. Except for Martine, who stood there with her hands on her hips.

"These pants are too tight to roll up," she grumbled.

"Then just go in with them on then, it won't hurt them to get wet," Janice snorted.

But Martine was not about to ruin her pants. She unzipped them and drew them down, then sat down on a log to pull them off, one leg at a time.

"Martine, don't," I pleaded.

"*Et alors*, who is going to see me?"

Just then we heard the sound of a truck coming down the path. It was one of the white pickup trucks the maintenance crews drove, the only vehicles allowed in the forest. This is what the driver must have seen: four mismatched women with two dogs, in various stages of undress. One short, blond, and built like a Shetland pony, stepping barelegged out of her jeans; one a tall, top-heavy redhead

with thin English skin and thin lips, holding a cocker spaniel on a leash; a younger woman with a pony tail, carrying
a whimpering mutt; and a smaller woman with dark brown
hair, looking at the truck with a hopeful expression.

"Martine, put your pants back on!" I urged. "Maybe
he'll stop and give us a ride across the bridge."

"He's more likely to do that if I don't put my pants back
on, *non?*"

But the truck kept coming at us, and splashed right past
us; whether the driver was oblivious to our predicament or
embarrassed by Martine's state of undress, we would never
know.

We often left the beaten path and took small footpaths
barely marked by the crushed undergrowth along the creek.
There were other hazardous crossings, over large drainage
pipes, logs, or rocks, and at such times I found myself wondering what I was doing in the woods, risking life and limb,
when I didn't even have a dog to walk or corporate politics
to play. I was the odd woman in the group, the only one who
did not have a husband working for the French multinational pharmaceutical company in Research Triangle Park.
Martine's husband, Jean-Marie, and Janice's husband, Larry,
were vying for the top spot, director of U.S. operations.
Penny's husband, Rob, reported to Jean-Marie, but Penny
seemed to have thrown in her lot with her fellow Englishwoman Janice.

I was there, I suppose, as a French-speaking counterbal-
ance of sorts on Martine's side; the first year, especially, she
often needed me to interpret for her. We tended to walk two
abreast, changing partners every so often over the course of
the one-and-one-half-hour walk.

We talked about children, dogs, and the vicissitudes of expatriate living in America, on which I was the resident expert, having lived here for so long. I had had my own year of first times when we moved to North Carolina: the first time I called out a man's name, and he, even before turning around, responded with that reflexive "ma'am?" that made me envy Southern mothers; the first time someone asked me what I was hunting and if they could carry me where I was going; the first time I stepped out of an air-conditioned house and the air outside slapped me in the face like a warm, wet washcloth; the first time I knew there was such a thing as a hurricane season.

The others had all arrived in Chapel Hill in the fall of 1995 when their husbands were relocated to RTP from Europe. I had met Martine in Lyon the previous summer, and when she came to North Carolina it was natural that she would look me up. On our walks, I was the one who knew why everything, from the hundreds of acres of forest to the university, from the hospital to the power company, was called Duke. I knew about—but could not actually identify in nature—poison oak and poison sumac. I could recognize—but could not actually explain—the arcane rites of those fearsome tribes, American high school students.

Mostly we talked about our children and dogs. Janice, who was the only one of us who had not gone to "uni," as she called it, reported on the progress of her son and daughter at expensive boarding schools back in England. Martine's children, who were roughly the same age as my son, were trying to adjust to Chapel Hill High and ESL (English as a Second Language) classes. I tried to help by pointing out the unspoken rule of never wearing the same outfit twice in the same week, and stressing the importance of joining a team sport. My son, Sherif, ran cross-country, one of the few sports that did not require tryouts, but the Grivotet kids couldn't see the point.

Penny, who was a few years younger than the rest of us, had children in middle and elementary schools. The children were fitting in smoothly, but Penny worried about her dog, Lizzie, who was old and decrepit; if they had to return to England, Lizzie would never survive the quarantine mandatory for canines entering the UK.

"We'll have to put her to sleep," she fretted. "The children will be so upset, Jeremy especially, he's the sensitive one. Oh well, we'll worry about it when the time comes." Jeremy was her eldest, a gifted and sweet-natured boy, by all accounts, and she had great ambitions for him.

Walking and talking, week in and week out, we trekked through the woods, measuring time by the rhythm of the seasons and the school year. Measuring the passing of the years by the forgiving computation of our children's open-ended lives rather than the narrowing gage of our own. The emerald sea of spring with its vicious yellow pollen dust yielded to the endless, steamy, bug-ridden months and back to the russet and copper and gold of an Indian summer.

I wonder if, in a way, what kept us coming back together week after week was the need to affirm some value in the fleeting days by sharing our mundane routines. Children's doctor appointments and dogs' grooming salons, husbands' travel schedules and cholesterol levels, hairdresser visits and diet progress, no detail was too small to collect in the tight sieve of our chatter as we traipsed through mud and bracken.

One year there was a shocking rape at gunpoint in Duke Forest. Duke campus police and the Durham police immediately arrested a young man who was found leaving the forest and who seemed to fit the description given by the victim. His name and face had been flashed all over the evening news on television that night: a nineteen-year-old, former high school cross-country champion. When his photo flashed on the screen, I called to my son in his room: could that be the boy who had been captain of the cross-country team the year Sherif started high school? I remembered seeing him at meets, running effortlessly ahead of the pack, his long blond hair streaming behind him. It was the same boy, my son confirmed, but Sherif, and everyone who remotely knew that boy, insisted that it must be a case of mistaken identity.

The boy's parents—physicians and prominent pillars of the community—used their influence to rush the DNA testing, and he was conclusively exonerated within weeks. But precious time had been lost, and any leads to the real perpetrator had gone cold. So the real rapist was "still out there." My walking companions on the Duke Forest treks congratulated themselves that they never walked there alone, but I argued that, since the woman had been raped while walking with two men and a dog, there really was no safety in numbers. Sociability would have to suffice as an end in itself.

After our walks we had breakfast together, each one hosting in turn. "Comfort after effort," Jean-Marie dubbed our late morning collations. There was a protocol to these breakfasts: coffee prepared in a French press, not in a drip coffee machine; croissants, toast, butter, and imported jam.

"I'm going for a mammogram this afternoon," Janice confided one morning when we were all sitting around the kitchen table at my house, watching the dogs panting in harmony out on the deck. "The nurse said I wasn't due for one till April but I thought I felt something in the shower this morning, and I'm not taking any chances, am I? My mum died at fifty of breast cancer, and our Jean had to have a radical mastectomy last year. Oh, speaking of bosoms, did you hear the Bob and Madison show on the radio this morning? Honestly, I don't know how they can get away with it!"

Janice seemed to listen to the radio and watch the "telly" a good deal, afternoon talk shows especially; she had no children at home and Larry was often away. I met Larry infrequently. Not having a husband with the firm—I was divorced—I didn't socialize with the others when they got together as couples for drinks or a cookout almost every weekend.

I passed the rolls and toast around but Penny shook her head. "No thanks, I'm not having any. I'm starting a diet. Is that coffee steeped yet?"

"Diet? Whatever for?" I pushed the plunger down in the French press. Penny was attractive in a hearty, sporty way, not the type to worry about a few extra pounds.

"Rob's started on this diet, see. We've both put on a few pounds since we got here. I mean, it's all this easy living, and all these big meals and wine with every meal! Even when we're on our own we've been having a bottle with dinner. So Rob says he's going on the Atkins diet, and at first I didn't think he'd stick with it, but he has, hasn't he; lost fourteen pounds in six weeks! So it's time I do something."

I wondered if Penny was feeling threatened, or just competitive. I could see that Rob could be attractive, with his easygoing smile and tall, loose frame.

"Well, then that's more croissants for me," Martine teased as she helped herself. Martine was atypical for a Frenchwoman in that she had a stocky build and no qualms about it. Jean-Marie, on the other hand, was deceptively small and wiry, a skilled mountain climber and outstanding downhill skier. But I could see that he might not be built to the scale of this new country where everything was supersized, from the cars to the drive-through drinks.

"So when will Jean-Marie be back from Lyon?" I asked Martine.

"Not till Friday," she sighed. "I'm waiting for him to come back to speak to Thibault and Chlöé about their studies. It's not the American high school that's the problem; it's getting them to study for the French Bac by correspondence courses."

As soon as they left I loaded the dishes in the dishwasher and hurried upstairs to my computer. One thing I didn't disclose to my walking companions was my all-consuming occupation for the balance of my hours alone at home. I was writing a novel. How do you end a relationship? How do you end a relationship that never existed, as far as the world knew? How do you achieve closure, that word I still see in quotation marks? You turn the page, you close the book. So many metaphors to remind you that writing can be just that: embalming the past in reams of paper and burying it between two covers. There is a neat finality to the sound of it but the actual process is as painful as plucking stingers out of your flesh. For me, each sting I plucked out represented a date: the date we met, an approximate date, because its significance wasn't clear to me yet; my birthday; his; the day and night we were happy; the day we parted; the day we reunited; the day we parted, again. Slowly, one by one, I plucked out the stings, killing a memory each time.

But I never mentioned a word about my writing to my walking companions. I explained my morbid secrecy to myself as an atavistic Eastern superstition: talking about something before it was a done deal would jinx it. Also, with many a slip between cup and lip, between pen and publication, I wanted to avoid the inevitable well-meaning questions about my progress. I didn't want to have to keep repeating, like Michelangelo painting the Sistine Chapel, that I would be done when I was finished. Besides, I reasoned, my walking companions would not be interested in the kind of writing I do. They all shared a passion for Mary Higgins Clark, even Martine, who read her in the French translation.

The September of the year Hurricane Fran struck, all our lives were put on hold for weeks. When we thought of resuming our walks again, after Christmas vacation, we looked around for alternative venues. Duke Forest was closed to the public, the paths blocked by the massive trunks of fallen trees. We tried walking in the woods not far from Governor's Club, where Janice and Larry leased a large house.

At our breakfasts now Penny touched nothing but black coffee and half a slice of plain toast. She was visibly melting away week by week, and we all envied her out loud and bemoaned our own lack of willpower to follow her example. She was also acquiring a splendid tan from boating on Jordan Lake in a bikini, and Janice teased her about having a touch of the tar brush.

"I know," Penny nodded. "Jeremy walked into the bedroom when I'd just come out of the shower, and he turned his head away and said, 'Mum, you should close the door when you're not decent!' But then he added, 'you're not half brown!'" She sounded half in love with her teenage son, the way most mothers are with sons on the threshold of manhood, I suppose.

By the spring after Hurricane Fran, we had started up our walks in Duke Forest again, even though it was still officially closed. The massive trunks and logs had been cleared from the main paths, but the tracks of devastation were everywhere, and crews were still clearing large swaths. But forests recover, we were told; they come back stronger than ever; within a few years of replanting no trace of the passage of Fran would be noticeable. The deer had thrived, as they prefer the edges of woods to deep forest; now we often had to leash Charlie to prevent him from giving chase—Lizzie, of course, was too old and too blind to be a threat.

Janice and Larry were building a six-bedroom house in a new subdivision in the suburb of Cary, a town twenty minutes away dubbed "containment area for relocated Yankees" for its high percentage of corporate transplants from the Northeast. They had chosen a development carefully carved into subdivisions designed, down to the lawn edgings, to reflect corporate hierarchy: a place for everyone and everyone in his place. You knew instantly where any resident stood on the game board of Snakes and Ladders. Larry and Janice's three-story new house was going up on one of the lots overlooking the golf course—the last square on the board.

"But the lot is so narrow, I can look into the neighbors' window as easily as I could in our little house in Ipswich,

I swear," Janice grumbled. "Easier, because there are no hedges or trees. They've cleared all the trees on the lot. It feels like five degrees hotter than in Chapel Hill. Oh well, it'll be nice when all the family come over from the UK for Christmas. And for when the kids bring their friends from college. Suppose I'd better start buying some furniture."

I glanced at Martine, who had made no comment. Jean-Marie had refused to buy a house, or even to rent a more imposing one than the modest ranch on a large wooded lot they had been renting for three years. Either Larry was more confident of his chances of being appointed director for U.S. operations, or he was positioning himself to appear that way. On the surface everyone acted like good friends, although the stakes were high. If Jean-Marie lost, Martine had confided to me, he would not work under Larry; he would ask to be transferred and take a demotion if need be.

Janice invited us to a luncheon at the Cary country club with the theme of "The Meaning of Being Southern." That, apparently, had everything to do with pecans, judging by the menu: honey-roasted pecans with the mint julep, followed by mixed-greens salad with pecans, cranberry/pecan bread, pecan-encrusted salmon, and pecan pie. We were also initiated into the southern wedding traditions of the groom's cake; the custom of choosing the father of the groom as best man; and the importance of selecting the right silver and china patterns.

But lessons in assimilation apart, Janice and Penny remained staunch Brits at heart. When Princess Diana was killed, they woke up at dawn to watch the funeral live on television. They had had no use for Tony Blair in general, but approved of the way he handled Diana's death, and were highly critical of the queen. The topic dominated our walks for a few weeks, but we rarely discussed serious politics or international issues. The only time I remember, we ended up arguing: Janice, and by extension Penny, were all for sanctions and bombing Iraq, regardless of civilian suffering, on the basis that the Iraqis deserved it for not ousting Saddam; Martine and I took the opposing point of view.

The seasons turned, and my son and Martine's Thibault and Chlöé were graduating from high school. Four years had passed, unbelievably. It was prom time. Martine, but also the Englishwomen, were scandalized at the fuss and expense of an American high school prom, the hundreds of dollars to rent tuxes and limos, the corsages and the gifts and the restaurants. I kept them entertained during our walks with reports of the prom date game, conducted over a ricochet of phone calls by Sherif and his friends. For three days I was required to stand duty by the telephone: if it was Elisabeth, I was to answer that my son was available; if it was Lauren, that I would check to see; if it was Lori, that he was out.

Martine's son went with a visiting French friend and her daughter with a Nigerian boy from ESL classes. The afternoon of the prom, Chlöé and the French friend went to the Lancôme counter at the mall to take advantage of an advertised free makeover, thinking it would be a brilliant ploy to have their makeup done expertly without having to buy anything. They came back red-faced; the makeup artist had only done half their faces, so they had to wipe it all off.

My son's date, in the event, was none of the girls he'd called or who called him, but a fellow runner, a girl on the cross-country team. That year, the team had chosen for their motto Nietzsche's "That which does not kill us only makes us stronger." The words resonated with me. I understood the celebration of graduation, the sheer relief of getting through four years of cliques, cabals, and subtle cruelties. The kids had survived American high school.

That summer the decision was taken. Larry had landed the prize; he would be the new head of the American operation of the multinational pharmaceutical company. Jean-Marie was out, and the Grivotets would be relocated back to Europe. Martine was disappointed, naturally, but seemed to be making the best of it. "We really miss family life, you know, the real family life we have in France; dinners together, conversation around the table. Here the kids were getting wild; we were feeling that we were losing control."

The Grivotets left at the end of the month; Janice and Larry gave a big farewell party for them at which I was the only guest not affiliated with the firm. I was also the only one without a husband in attendance, but Larry and Rob made up for it by being unusually attentive, so much so that a colleague of Rob's mistook me for his wife; Penny said she didn't mind sharing for one evening.

We went on with our walks, without Martine. Penny ran for five miles before our walks now. She was starting to look pinched, almost anorexic. She didn't bring Lizzie any more; the dog was getting too slow to keep up, and half blind. Penny fretted more than ever about what to do with Lizzie if they had to go back to the UK. "The vet says the trip would do her in, let alone the quarantine. And she's too old and confused to be given to anyone. I'd rather put her to sleep. Either way, it'll kill Jeremy."

Janice, for her part, seemed uncharacteristically glum. The first time we had breakfast at her new house, I asked her if she wanted to go furniture shopping in High Point. "No, I think I'm going to hold off that for a while."

"How did your biopsy go?" I asked. Janice had check-ups twice a year and the last had indicated a lump; she'd gone in to have a biopsy over the weekend.

"There was a lump, wasn't there, so they took it out when they did the biopsy, I'd said going in that I wanted it done. So now we'll wait for the results. I expect I shall have to have a mastectomy sooner or later though, with my family history. Oh, honestly, Nadia," she added when she saw the expression on my face, "You do what you need to carry on, don't you."

I had more time to write now; with my son away at college, the fumes of testosterone and restlessness had cleared from the house. I passed Sherif's outgrown dress blazer and pants to Penny for Jeremy to wear.

One Wednesday morning the news of the buyout of the pharmaceutical company made the front page of the *Raleigh News and Observer.* The rumors had been floating around for weeks, but there had periodically been so many I had paid no attention. I wondered if Janice and Penny would show up for our walk that day, but when I drove up to Duke Forest their minivans were parked by the entrance as usual. The two women seemed resigned, as if they had been expecting the news. Janice put the new house on the market, but in any case the company would take it off their hands if they couldn't sell it themselves.

In the event, Larry was hired by another multinational and was relocated to Geneva; he took Rob along. We walked sporadically those last few weeks; Janice and Penny were busy with packing and making relocating arrangements.

There was some tension between the two of them; Penny wanted Rob's relocation package to pay for a private boarding school for Jeremy. After considerable wrangling she got her way, and Jeremy left ahead of the rest of the family to start summer camp at his new school in the Alps.

A week later Janice called to tell me that Jeremy had dropped dead, literally—incredibly—while hiking in the mountains with his camp mates and counselors. Rob had driven over immediately from Geneva but there was nothing he could do. Penny and the younger children were flying out the very same day, and Janice would join them. Would I take care of Lizzie? Of course I would. Janice dropped off Lizzie and her paraphernalia an hour later on her way to the airport.

I called Martine; Jean-Marie was already on the road, driving to the camp from Lyon. Jeremy had always been so healthy and athletic; how could this have happened? Had there been a congenital weakness of the heart? But we were talking in circles; there was nothing to say. You hear about unspeakable tragedies but you never believe it could happen to someone you know. You never believe it can happen to you. Of all the nightmare scenarios we could have contemplated on our long walks, the loss of a child was the one eventuality too terrible to imagine. There was nothing to say; you couldn't say it could have been worse. Or so I thought at the time, but today I've revised my opinion.

I saw Penny and Rob when they came back to take care of the final details of the move. She looked so thin and feverish and dry-eyed that I worried she wouldn't make it. Rob's concern for her overwhelmed his own feelings, mercifully perhaps for him. Penny went around searching for Jeremy in the faces of his schoolmates, his teachers, his coaches, the girl who was the closest thing to a girlfriend he had had at fifteen. Penny collected their memories of Jeremy as if she were afraid a single detail would slip through the sieve.

The autopsies had revealed nothing: no congenital defect, no hereditary risk factor, nothing Jeremy's two younger siblings might be tested for. Nothing. As I hugged Penny goodbye, a window cracked open in the brittle wall around her. She met my eyes. "I don't see how people who don't have other children carry on living after something like this."

I wrote Penny and Rob a letter after they left. I remember I said, "You haven't lost Jeremy. You will find Jeremy always, everywhere you go, and one day you will see him in the faces of your grandchildren."

The following year I spent part of the summer in Europe, as I usually did, and spent a few days with the Grivotets near Lyon; I took the high-speed TGV train down from Paris on a lovely summer day. Thibault picked me up at La Part Dieu station in his mother's car.

That evening, after dinner, I took a shower and curled up in my bathrobe on the living room sofa, listening to *Carmina Burana* with Jean-Marie while Martine answered the telephone in the kitchen. I asked Jean-Marie how he felt about taking early retirement in a year and he interrupted me with, "Don't you think it's about time we dropped the formal *vous*?"

I caught sight of myself in the mirror with my head wrapped in a towel and laughed. "High time!"

Martine came in with a big smile. "I have a surprise for you. Guess who is coming to visit on Friday? Penny! She's driving down from Geneva for the day just to see us."

Penny had put on some weight and looked more like I remembered her when she first arrived in the United States. She had also regained her even, almost cheery, manner, perhaps a little quieter than before. We went to a restaurant called Les Glycines for lunch, and Penny and I opted for sitting outside under the wisteria-covered pergola.

"But the scent of the *glycines* could overpower the food," Martine grumbled. "Wisteria? Is that what you call it in English? It sounds like a disease!"

"And glycine sounds like an ointment!"

I don't remember what we had, except for the little balls of blood pudding we were served as appetizer, because I had popped one in my mouth before I realized what they were. I only remember that it was a day when it was particularly good to feel alive. We didn't speak of Jeremy. But I knew Penny had made it through a year: Jeremy's birthday; the first Christmas without him; the first family card signed without his name; the first vacation; the first beginning of the school year. A year of dates. She would have to brace herself, probably all her life, when certain dates came around on the calendar. But she'd made it through the first year; she would make it through the next.

We spoke of Lizzie. Penny had taken her with her to Switzerland after all, and she had survived the trip. She spent her time sitting on a blanket now, blind and incontinent, but still there. We spoke of Janice; she was in the Bahamas with Larry at the moment, but another biopsy hung over her head when she returned. "It's like Russian roulette with me," she'd told me once. "If it's not sooner it will be later."

We said good-bye, without speaking of Jeremy. I could see that the wall around Penny had no window for me.

of love, or the death of ambition; to find the will to live with the loss of a limb, or the loss of a child; to outlive the loss of innocence. That which does not kill us—unless, of course, it kills us first.

That fall my book was published, and more friends
I knew I had came to the first reading. None of the wa[l]
group was there, of course, but they all read it. I still [h]
in touch with the Grivotets regularly, and occasionally
them in Europe. The last time I was in London, Janice an[d]
went to the matinee of a play in Leicester Square and out
dinner together.

Right after September 11 happened, the Grivotets calle[d]
to urge me to come visit them in France, to "change the atmosphere," as they put it. I told them not to worry, that I was all
right. Janice and Penny sent Christmas cards with photos.
The last one from Janice showed her looking splendid in a
big peach hat at her daughter's wedding.

I still walked in Duke Forest alone, although I carried a
cell phone with me. Then one morning, in the Chapel Hill
newspaper, I saw that boy's name and face again, the former
cross-country runner who had been falsely accused of the
rape at Duke Forest. This time the paper was reporting that
he had taken his own life, suddenly, inexplicably, nearly eight
years after the incident. Eight years of leading a productive,
ostensibly well-adjusted existence. Eight years of searching
for the shadow of lingering doubt in other people's eyes.

My first thought was for his parents. I had thought that
nothing could be worse than losing a child the way Penny
had, but now I know there is worse. Having your child take
his own life is worse.

I thought of the cross-country team's motto the year my
son was a senior in high school: "that which does not kill
us only makes us stronger." How many of us, faced with a[n]
unbearable trauma, have to kill something in ourselves t[o]
carry on with what is left of our lives? To survive the deat[h]

Muslims in the Cul-de-sac

In the rhythm of the seasons, fall is the true beginning of the year in a college town. In the South, in particular, the cooler, crisper breezes of September dispel the lethargy of the long, muggy summer months, and the bustle of returning students jolts the sleepy downtown streets back to life. Just as the song of the scarlet cardinals heralds the renewal of spring, the influx of students pouring into campus heralds a new academic year.

So it was always in September that I organized my annual open house in the college town I had called home for ten years. A "wine and heavy hors d'oeuvres" affair, it was an occasion to reconnect with a diverse group of returning summer wanderers: colleagues from the university and the local newspaper, French and Francophile friends from conversation groups. I invited about thirty people, no RSVP required, and estimated that about twenty-five would show up.

That September of the first year of the new millennium, my only source of concern was the weather: a friend had offered to help with landscaping the yard, and as it turned out, could only do it on the day of the party itself, a Saturday. "Don't worry," Karen reassured me. "It will all be done before your guests arrive at seven." I wondered if she had bitten off more than she could chew. The previous weekend, a mound of mulch as high as the house had been delivered and sat in my driveway, and bushes in canvas sacks lined the path to the front door. If it rained before Saturday, there would be an unholy mess.

As I checked my e-mail the Tuesday before the party, I kept glancing out the window at the pile of mulch and at the sky, praying the good weather would last through the weekend. A box suddenly opened on my screen, flashing what looked like a trailer for a disaster movie: black smoke pouring out of tall buildings. Then the phone rang. "Turn on the television," a friend instructed grimly. The World Trade Center towers had been attacked.

My first thought was for my older son, who regularly had business in downtown New York. I couldn't reach him. My second thought was to pray that the perpetrators, as it turned out with the Oklahoma bombing, were not from the Middle East. My third thought was for the friends who had children or relatives in New York, and I tried to call them.

When it seemed increasingly likely that the hijackers were Middle Eastern, my reaction was to get up, tidy the house, and do the laundry. That instinct, I realize now, was more atavistic than rational. Growing up in Egypt, whenever there was a national catastrophe like the 1967 defeat, my father and uncles packed their overnight bags, preparing to be hauled away by the Intelligence Service, the Mukhabarat, simply because they were on the list of "enemies of the people."

I didn't pack an overnight bag, but I prepared for some inchoate eventuality: that our house would be searched by the FBI, or that neighbors might come to the door. It seemed important for everything to be tidy and clean, laundry done and put away, the house presentable, ready for inspection. As if, from that moment on, I had lost the right to privacy, the right not to be judged as a representative of a perceived "community."

I told my younger son to pick up his room and take down his laundry. For once, he obeyed without question, and the full significance of that struck me later.

As I picked up the books trailing about all over the house and stuffed them back on the shelves, I turned the spines of the few books in Arabic toward the bookcase.

But at least having something with which to occupy myself broke the unbearable paralysis that bound me to the television set and the telephone. When my older son finally called—from Hong Kong, as it happened—I breathed again. But then my thought was for the mothers who did not receive that reassuring phone call.

There was no knock on the door, either from police or neighbors, not that day nor the days that followed. There was a phone call from a French journalist in New York; she had been sent to cover the attack on the towers and to wrap up her coverage with a report from "heartland America." We had French friends in common who had suggested Chapel Hill as a location and gave her my number as a local contact. I said I would help any way I could. She would be arriving Saturday.

Saturday! The day of the open house party. Should I cancel? But how? I had invited people weeks ahead, and since I had not asked for an RSVP, I had no idea who might actually attend. I contemplated calling one by one everyone I had invited and disinviting them, but I couldn't remember everybody. What would it look like to the neighbors if

I held a party—to which none of them, incidentally, had been invited? Not that I didn't get along with the neighbors, only that we had little in common and didn't socialize. For one thing, my children were grown, and most of the families in the cul-de-sac had bought their houses from the original owners and had much younger children; the turnover was pretty high among families of young professionals, what with the booming economy of Research Triangle Park nearby.

I worried that a frenzy of landscaping and partying would look to the neighbors at the very least like ghastly insensitivity to the terrible events earlier that week. I worried and worried, but given the impracticality of canceling, I finally decided to go ahead, expecting that few people would show up anyway, if for no other reason than because they were in no mood to tear themselves away from the horror show that was our television screens.

Every time the phone rang I wondered if it would be someone calling to cancel or to confirm, but there were neither. There was a call, out of the blue, from the parents of a college friend of my son's, a successful, jolly couple, also one of the most fervently Christian families I knew. The parents, whom we'd only met a couple of times at college events, were calling to let us know that if we felt in any way threatened or uncomfortable, we were welcome to stay at their beach house for as long as we liked. We reassured them that there was no cause for concern. Their genuine kindness touched me to tears, but the—justifiable—assumption behind the gesture depressed me.

Saturday morning Karen showed up with her sleeves rolled up and a couple of men to do the heavy lifting. I pitched in, ineffectively, and she chased me indoors to set up for the party. The pile of mulch gradually diminished, as the neighbors went about their weekend business, eyeing the activity with curious glances.

But I had a strategy: to corner Gwen, my neighbor across the street, the only survivor, other than me, of the original residents of the cul-de-sac when it was a new subdivision ten years earlier. It wouldn't be hard to run into Gwen; she made it her business to know what was going on, perhaps in her capacity as doyenne of the neighborhood. Gwen and her husband, a researcher in physics at the university, were childless, but she always had a reason to hang about her front yard, and you could hear her speaking to various neighbors, mailmen, and delivery people in a Minnesota accent that carried effortlessly clear across the entire block.

Gwen could be counted on to relay any information you wished to publicize. So the Saturday of the party, I saw her taking her time looking through her mail at the bottom of her driveway, and went over and explained that the landscaping, and the party, had been planned a month ago and that I had no way of canceling. She nodded encouragingly. Message delivered.

A quarter of an hour before the guests arrived, Karen packed up her gear and her crew and left, promising to come back when she had showered and changed.

The French journalist, whom I had invited, was the first to arrive, a little before seven: a thirtysomething brunette, wearing combat boots with her denim skirt; perhaps she had prepared for ground zero, or perhaps it was just urban chic. We discussed various venues where I could help her set up interviews: Duke University, where I taught at the time;

the newspaper where I contributed a weekly book review column; the sole Afghan restaurant in the area, Bread and Kebabs.

"Oh, and tomorrow is Sunday, I would like to attend a service at a Protestant church. It must be a *Protestant* church," Valérie—that was her name—stressed.

"What kind of Protestant church?" I asked.

Just then the doorbell rang. I looked at my watch: it was seven fifteen. Joan, an old friend, walked through the open door carrying a paper bag of the latest overflow from her vegetable garden. Valérie jumped up and stuck a small mike in her face. "Hi! I'm Valérie. I'm doing a *reportage* on the reaction to the attacks. May I ask where were you when you heard?"

Joan recoiled. I apologized and asked Valérie not to ambush my guests that way. By seven thirty people began to arrive in clusters, and by eight there were thirty-five people hanging about the kitchen and the living room and over-flowing onto the deck. Some of my friends, bless them, had even brought friends of theirs along. I was still too unused to the new order of things to fully appreciate their kindness.

Before she left I asked Valérie if she had any particular denomination of Protestant church in mind for the Sunday service and she said no, just Protestant. I asked her to come by the next morning at eleven and we went to attend the service at the brand new Evangelical church down the street. It was a convenient five-minute walk away and it fulfilled her criterion. For weeks I had seen the posters advertising the grand opening on Sunday, September 16.

Valérie was visibly impressed as we walked across the vast parking lot to the front of the enormous, circular edifice that could be mistaken for a sports stadium. Inside she was even more taken aback by the raised sound stage on which a band of musicians was tuning up while a giant screen overhead projected video clips of young evangelists on their missions—the church catered mostly to university students. I talked to the pastor, a good-looking, fortysomething man with a resolutely cheerful manner, and he promised an interview for Valérie after the service. We took our seats in the front row of the stadium-style circular benches.

I had brought a hat with me, but no one else was wearing one, so I kept it in my lap; the woman sitting behind me leaned forward and whispered archly, "Pretty hat; but if you want to wear that, you'll have to go to a black church."

"Qu'est-ce qu'elle dit?" Valérie hissed; fluent in English though she was, Southern accents foiled her. But she switched on her little tape recorder and recorded it all, the music and the clapping and the dancing, and the solemn moment when the pastor asked everyone assembled to stand up and hold hands and pray—for victory for the university's football team that season. We were all at the time, I realize now, still in the denial stage of grief.

But as the weeks turned into months, denial turned to anger. In the battery of fun-house images of Islam that blared from television, radio, and newspaper headlines, I could not recognize the faith with which I was raised. Wherever I turned, it was bewildering and inescapable. When it became unbearable, I knew I needed to act. If you had a choice—and I did—you could keep a low profile and blend in as you always had, or you could stand up and speak out. I think my choice was decided from the moment I told my son to pick up his room and he obeyed without question.

I called the librarian at the town library, where I had recently been invited to give a reading for my first novel, and offered to give a talk about Islam. She discussed it with the board and called me back to say that they would take me up on my offer and would schedule me for the Sunday after next, as part of their regular "Meet the Author" events; except, she stressed, that they would not be serving the usual coffee and cookies. I understood perfectly: they could not be seen as in any way endorsing whatever it was I had to say.

In the event, even without the lure of refreshments, sixty people showed up for my talk, a record for the Sunday series, and the session ran well over the allotted time. Questions ran the gamut from genuine curiosity to barely disguised hostility. At the conclusion I felt that at least no one had left with a worse impression than they had when they arrived, and several people came up to me and asked if I would speak at their church.

I think it must have been the third or fourth church—invariably a Presbyterian congregation—at which I was speaking when I caught sight of my neighbor Gwen in the audience; she actually seemed to duck when I tried to make eye contact. After the talk I caught her at the coatrack by the door.

"Why Gwen, is this your church?"

"No, I go to the Lutheran church. But I'm in charge of Adult Education programs for my church and I'm organizing a series of speakers on Islam, so I came to hear you. Actually I didn't know it was you, just that they would have a Muslim speaker. I didn't know we had Muslims in the cul-de-sac!"

And there it was, the phrase I was to remember so often afterward: Muslims in the cul-de-sac.

"But Gwen, we've been neighbors for eight years, what did you think we were?"

"I don't know. But I didn't think you were that sort of Muslim!"

What sort of Muslim did she mean? The type, presumably, who didn't wear shorts and a tank top to water the bushes, and didn't have parties after which the recycle bin put out on the curb was full of empty wine bottles? But I never found out what she meant. Other people were edging around to ask me questions, and she left.

Gwen came to my door the next day with a stack of magazines. "Do you know this magazine?" She held up a magazine called *Aziza* with an African American woman in a headscarf on the cover.

"No, I don't actually."

"Oh, I thought you would. It's for Muslim women. I've been subscribing to it for a few weeks now, since I'm organizing the speaker series on Islam."

I thought of our African American mailman with his habitual smile, and how it must confuse him to deliver *Aziza* magazine to Gwen Stevenson. I asked her to come in. She had only been in my house once before, to an open house I gave when we first moved in, but as she never reciprocated, I didn't repeat the invitation. But after that terrible September, whenever Gwen, or anyone for that matter, came to my door, I invited them in: I felt an obligation to show that my life was an open book.

Over the next couple of weeks Gwen came many times with questions about Islam, and to ask for advice about speakers. So far she had invited only non-Muslim scholars of religion; she was ready to take the next step and invite a

Muslim to speak, but was worried about some nasty e-mail from members of her congregation accusing her of wanting to bring terrorists to the church.

Gwen finally went ahead and invited me to her church—but not to her home. That was to happen much later, and it was to be the first and the last time.

For Gwen's sake, I hope I did a good job of my presentation before her congregation that day; it seemed to go smoothly enough. I remember one man who kept mentioning that I had soft hands, which baffled me until I understood he was trying to make the point that he had shaken hands with me earlier, in contravention to what he had apparently been told to expect from Muslim women.

These talks I gave, sometimes as often as twice a week, were a strain, but I welcomed them for the temporary relief from helplessness they provided. Like many people, I lost a year of my life, numbly watching the Home and Garden channel or the Food Network when I could no longer bear the news channels. I wanted my old life back.

Pulling in and out of our driveway became fraught with a certain tension. I realized that I had been guilty of the one failing people rarely forgive: lack of curiosity about them. I had been the kind of oblivious neighbor who pulls into and out of her garage with her mind on other things, barely sparing a distracted glance for who might be about or what was going on. Now I noticed everything. The neighbors didn't wave, but then perhaps they never had? The children in particular seemed sullen and suspicious as they paused in their pick-up ball games to let my car through; but perhaps that was my imagination? The minor sources of friction—inconsiderate neighbors who let their dogs mess in our yard, or blew their leaves onto our lawn, or parked on the curb in front of our mailbox, blocking the postman's access—I let it all go. Perhaps I would have anyway.

That was around the time Attorney General John Ashcroft encouraged Americans, as a civic duty, to spy on "suspicious" neighbors, and mailmen, gas meter readers, and other utility workers were exhorted to take advantage of their access and snoop about the premises. I never seriously considered that any of my neighbors, not even the least friendly, and certainly not our smiling, long-time mailman, would be that paranoid.

Before the invasion of Iraq, Gwen came around again for one of our sessions. She asked me if it was possible the Iraqi people might welcome the invasion, given how much they must hate Saddam. I thought of the Suez crisis of 1956; at the time Egypt was attacked, if anyone had a reason to wish for the toppling of Nasser's regime and the restoration of the status quo ante, it would have been my father: the coup d'état of the colonels had stripped his family of its fortunes and his eldest brother was imprisoned. But my father was a nationalist; far from harboring the hope that the invasion would succeed, he volunteered for civil defense. I didn't go into all that with Gwen, needless to say.

One day Gwen waylaid me as I was pulling into my driveway. But this time she didn't have a question about Islam or Iraq; she wanted to tell me that she was getting divorced from her husband of eighteen years. I was touched, and surprised, that I was the one she chose to confide in; it had never occurred to me that, in her own way, she might be as isolated in the cul-de-sac as I was.

For a while things were rough for her, and she put on what looked like thirty pounds overnight. I tried to keep an open door for her whenever she came around to unburden herself over a cup of coffee. It took nearly two years for her to get her life together again and relaunch her career, but she finally found a job in Minneapolis and put her house across the street from mine on the market. Before she left she had a farewell party for neighbors, friends, even her ex-husband. She invited me and I was glad I was between trips abroad at the time and able to attend.

Now that Gwen has moved away, there is no one among the neighbors with whom I exchange more than casual remarks about the weather or the odd recommendation for handymen and house painters. Ironic, isn't it, that now that Gwen is gone, I am the resident with the longest seniority in the cul-de-sac.

It's Not About That

It wasn't about that. It was never about that, between us, so when it did become about that? It was never about my being from Egypt and your being American, about our coming from opposite ends of the spectrum on almost every issue. A few months after we met, I wrote to you, "It's a miracle, that we come from worlds so far apart, and met the way we did, and connect the way we do." I saw the distance between us better than you could, because I could see your starting point as well as mine. Your world has always been part of mine, long before I became part of it. I grew up reading Jane Austen and watching *Bonanza* on television in Cairo. You grew up in Connecticut; you didn't grow up reading El-Mutanabi's poetry or watching Egyptian films starring Omar Sharif. We have different memories.

You remember where you were when you heard that President Kennedy had been shot; it was your freshman year at Harvard. You didn't enjoy college: you weren't athletic, you didn't get into the right clique. Maybe that's where you learned to make your credo: If you can't join them, beat them.

I remember where I was in 1967, when the Six-Day War broke out. It was June, and unusually hot, even for Cairo; I was sitting in the bathtub, studying for junior high finals, holding up my book to prevent it from slipping into the water.

139

I had my own system of mnemonics to memorize international treaties: Bismarck, Balfour Treaty, Pax Britannica.

Then the air raids over Cairo began. In the living room my father was listening to the radio. "Ten Israeli fighter planes shot down!" the announcer exulted. A few minutes later: "Five more planes down!" My father was looking grim.

"But that's good, isn't it, Papa?" I asked. "I mean, that we're shooting them down so fast?"

He looked at me impatiently, something he almost never did. "Use your head. If we're shooting down ten planes in ten minutes, how many must be coming at us at once?"

Then he saw the expression on my face and added, "Don't worry, the announcer is exaggerating, they always do. Let's try to get the BBC on the shortwave radio."

In those days, in Egypt, there was zero confidence in any announcement made by government officials—even about something as innocuous as the weather. The temperatures in summer seemed to be consistently underreported by several degrees, as though people could be manipulated into feeling the heat less, or as if they would blame the government for the weather.

You could be arrested for listening to shortwave radio, but we did it anyway. The Israelis were attacking with overwhelming force, and the Egyptian air force had been obliterated before it ever got off the ground.

We followed the blackout instructions, papering over our windowpanes with the navy wax paper with which we covered our copy books at school. I had stopped studying for finals completely, and so had all of my school friends. We were in a state of feverish excitement, waiting to be called upon to do something, we had no idea what. Only one girl in the class went right on studying. "Whether we win, or whether they do, there will be exams anyway. Even under enemy occupation, there will be exams eventually. And I'm going to be the only one who's prepared."

We looked at her the way you do when someone utters blasphemy or unspeakable obscenity.

The war was over almost as soon as it began. Israeli forces swallowed up the Sinai and stopped short just the other side of the Suez. When President Nasser announced the total defeat of our much-vaunted armies, we were disbelieving. We were so used to the spin, as you would call it today, that it was devastating to realize that this defeat was beyond even Nasser's ability to spin or obfuscate.

Later that year the song that was top of the pop charts all over the world went, "Those were the days my friend / We'd fight and never lose." We sang it over and over, stressing "we'd fight and never lose" defiantly; it could be construed as subversive. In those days, in Egypt, you had to watch what you said and did.

And you? Where were you in 1967? You were staying out of the Vietnam War. Vietnam was the war that defined your generation of Americans, and you were on the right side of the great moral divide of your country: you demonstrated against the war and for civil rights, you had black friends; you're still a card-carrying member of the ACLU.

I remember where I was when I heard that President Nasser had died in 1970. It was in the evening, and the maid came up to tell us she had heard on the street that the *rais* was dead. We warned her that she could get into trouble spreading rumors. I had been born under the Nasser regime, as had the overwhelming majority of Egyptians. No one could believe in his death. Television footage of his funeral showed scenes of mass hysteria. Even my father, who had suffered so much at Nasser's hands, was subdued. In Arab culture, you owe respect to death, not to the man; you walk in your enemy's funeral cortege.

In 1973, there was the October War, the Ramadan War we called it, while the other side called it Yom Kippur. I was in London at the time, studying at the university. At every church corner people were handing out flyers advertising "Come celebrate with the music of Handel's Israel in Egypt." At Hyde Park Speaker's Corner on Sunday the Arab students demonstrated at one end and the Israeli supporters at the other.

You had married and moved to Connecticut. Your first son was born, and you started to grow a beard. When I knew you, you had a full reddish beard. I asked you once if that was a Jewish tradition, to start growing a beard when your first son was born, and you said that's not why you did it, you were very secular.

I remember where I was when I heard that Sadat had been assassinated. It was 1981 and I was living in faculty housing on a Pennsylvania campus, with my husband and sons. I was nursing the baby as I watched the funeral on television. President Carter was there, and many other heads of state, paying their homage to Sadat, the martyr for peace. The Egyptian crowd was strangely subdued, the commentators noted, so unlike the scene at Nasser's funeral.

Did you watch the same coverage? Maybe not, you were busy building up your business then, with that single-mindedness I know so well. It must have taken its toll on your marriage. You didn't see as much of your children as you would have liked while they were growing up.

And me? The years passed and I blended into my new environment like a perfect chameleon. My sons grew up engrossed in Ninja Turtles cartoons and Transformer car-robots; they played hockey and soccer. There was no room in this brave new world for memories of Egypt.

By the time I met you, your days of itching ambition were behind you and success had mellowed you. You attended your college reunion and realized that you had been more popular than you remembered. The bar mitzvah you held for your son eclipsed those of everyone in your circle; you were very secular, but it wasn't about that.

When we met, it wasn't about what we were to the outside world. It wasn't about that, whatever it was. We each recognized something at the core of the other, and that flash of recognition, so rare, so blinding, made us discard all the rest as mere outer layers we didn't need.

I remember where we were when the market crashed on Black Monday. We were in your car, driving along some New England country road; you had the radio on, and you were following the free fall of the market. You took your hand off mine long enough to adjust the volume, then you found my hand again, palm against palm.

The first time we argued about international affairs was in a pub in a random small town along the route of one of our aimless drives in the country. When we pulled off the highway into the village, you said, "I wonder where the local watering hole is." Then you caught sight of a man shuffling along the sidewalk. "He looks like he'd know." You stuck your head out of the car window. "Sir? I say, where's the pub? The bar?"

I have a confession to make: I liked your sense of humor at times like that when you weren't trying to be funny; I didn't care as much for your jokes.

In the pub you had your beer and ham sandwich, and I had a glass of wine and picked at your chips. I liked to watch you eat; you ate recklessly for a man with a full beard. I liked to watch your eyes: intensely blue, deep-set, quizzical. You kept trying to make me have some fried clams. I was never hungry when we were together; I was either too happy or too miserable.

I don't remember what brought the conversation around to the Middle East, what set us off on that argument. It doesn't matter. That issue was like a nightmare merry-go-round; you could hop on at any juncture, but as soon as you tried to look behind you to see the starting point, or look ahead of you to the resolution, it all became a blur, and in the meantime the merry-go-round never stopped, the cycle of grievances went on and on, and all you could do was go round and round until you bailed out, dizzy and battered.

You liked the idea of me as your Arab *pasionaria,* one of the new roles I somehow found myself playing for you. You found conflict stimulating; I had no stomach for it, especially with you. I gave up without ceding, or you ceded under the unfair pretext of "make love, not war." But we agreed that we were two of the most open-minded, well-intentioned people we knew, and if we couldn't discuss this issue sanely, no one could.

That was our year of living dangerously. When we broke up, it wasn't about that, whatever it was.

In 1990, when the Gulf War started, we were very far apart, in every sense. I don't know if you watched Saddam Hussein's televised speech promising "the mother of all battles." Isn't it amazing how quickly that ancient Arabic expression—"mother of all something"—was adopted in

American everyday idiom? I hear and read it all the time now, used by people who don't even remember the context.

&⁊&⁊During Desert Storm, I thought, for the first time, of leaving the States. My sons, all of a sudden, became "Arabs" at school. It didn't matter that the Egyptians were fighting on the same side as the Allies. But the war ended almost as soon as it had begun, and we stayed.

I don't know what you were doing then, we had dropped off each other's radar completely. But I know you must have thought of me at the time. You always did, whenever there were reports of a hurricane devastating the Carolinas, or some other threat. The telephone would ring, the morning after some ice storm or hurricane, as I was clearing out the defrosted fridge or estimating the damage to the roof from fallen trees. I would pick up the receiver, and there would be silence at the other end. Then, after you heard my voice—it was you, wasn't it?—you'd click once, slowly, softly, like a kiss, and hang up.

Years later, we became friends, at a distance. Whatever brought us back in touch, it wasn't about that.

From a distance, then, we became friends. We shared what we could: opinions on books and music and current events. Those were the heady days when peace seemed at hand in the Middle East. You were more optimistic than I was; you believed human beings would ultimately act out of rational self-interest. One day you called me, elated: the orchestra at your alma mater was planning a "peace tour" of Egypt and Israel during spring break. I was just as thrilled. Then there was the massacre in a temple in Luxor, followed by the massacre in a mosque in Hebron, and the peace tour was canceled.

At some point we decided to risk a meeting, in the lounge of an airport in a city neither of us knew. I was looking around for you, but I didn't see you, or didn't recognize you, until you were standing right in front of me. It was your eyes I recognized first; your eyes were the same. You said I hadn't changed.

Before we parted, you said that you hadn't changed, about me, about us. If we were to stay no more than friends, it would have to be at a distance, it was too painful to try to do it a breath's length apart. It was your decision to make; I would have been willing to try.

When the millennium came around, we were as weary as the rest of the world with the eternal and insoluble problems of the Middle East. One day we were arguing over the phone when we came close to a meltdown. I was the one who saw the danger first and pulled back. This time there was no point in getting back on the merry-go-round. I'm not sure why it was different: whether we had changed, or whether the situation had become too hopeless and too volatile.

Afterward you wrote to me, "If two open-minded people like us can't discuss this issue sanely, no one can. You're mistaken if you think lack of communication brings us closer, in matters personal or political. That's not what intimacy or friendship are about."

I wrote back, "I want us to be friends. But there's so much space between us right now. Don't let's fill it with the crackle of brittle cerebral volleys. I don't want to argue with you. It makes me feel sad and hurt."

And you wrote, "Funny, I don't feel any space between us. Can there be one-sided space? Doesn't sound real. But I guess emotions and geometry are different."

But I stopped discussing Middle East affairs with you. The problem, you thought, was that there were too many facts to choose from. But I knew it went deeper than that; we had no memories in common. If we lost our friendship again, I didn't want it to be about that, whatever it was.

Like everyone else, we both know exactly where we were when we heard the World Trade Center Towers were attacked. I was checking my e-mail that Tuesday morning when the small box popped up on the screen, the box that typically features something like an image of a teenage pop idol and the caption "Britney Spears or Christina Aguilera: which is hotter? Click here." This time the box showed an image of the World Trade towers in flames and the caption "America Under Attack." I thought it was a commercial for the latest apocalyptic movie until someone called and told me to turn on the television set.

My first thought was to pray that my older son was not one of the victims—he regularly had business in Lower Manhattan at the time, as did yours. As soon as my son called to say he was all right, I called you; your son was safe as well.

I reached out to you at that moment, with everything I thought we had in common. You responded with a diatribe against all Muslims everywhere. I don't remember exactly what you said; after the first few words all I registered was my own pain. It's not that I didn't understand your reaction. If I had read your opinion in a newspaper as a letter to the editor from a stranger, I could have riposted, point for point, with equanimity. But coming from you, it undid me. I cried for a long time afterward, mourning someone I knew—or thought I knew—that I lost that awful day.

Almost immediately, you called. The best of us try to be better than their first instinct. You said you never meant for me to take what you said personally; that you were willing to put aside our differences for the sake of our friendship. I knew that. I knew you wouldn't hurt me for the world, not in cold blood.

It wasn't your fault, or mine. It's as if, overnight, a war had been declared across the world, and a wall came slamming down the middle, and innocent civilians were caught on either side. We found ourselves on opposite sides of a wall.

I told you I would always wish you well. But I wanted you to understand: we had nothing left to talk about. This time, it was about that.

Last Word

But it wasn't that cut and dried, was it. That wasn't the end.

No, it wasn't. You kept calling, even when I hung up on you. I couldn't bear to hear your voice, it hurt too much. I felt so betrayed. I wanted to erase everything you knew of me from your memory, everything you ever saw or touched or tasted; I wanted to take it all back. But you kept calling, leaving messages on the answering machine, or with anyone else who picked up. I didn't know how to explain them. That's blackmail, do you know that?

I needed to fix what was wrong between us. I needed to make sure of that before you left.

And before I left, we agreed on our rules of nonengagement. We couldn't argue about *that*. And we couldn't talk about us. But you said I had to keep writing to you; I could write about the rest. This time, you said, you wanted to understand.

And I try to. But memory is a strange thing . . . there are things I remember differently, in what you write.

"There is fiction in the space between / You, and me."

That's from a song by Tracy Chapman.

Rashômon. Do you know it? The film by Akira Kurosawa.

A much more elegant reference, thank you. But it's true, isn't it? No two people ever remember things exactly the same. And when you try to write it down, it's always fiction.

149

Even if every word happened, in the end, when you write it, it's fiction. Take that last story; it just seemed to write itself that way, it came full circle; the circle came to an end.

A circle has no beginning and no end, don't you know that?

Geometry and emotions are different things; didn't you say that?

Touché. So, in this circular argument of ours, are you staying? Are you coming back?

I don't know. Must I choose?

There is no wall, you know. We're on the same side.

But I feel like the lines have been drawn, and someone like me finds herself straddling the wall; it's a very uncomfortable position. But at least I can see both sides.

So you say. And this fiction of yours, what do you propose to call it?

How about *Lamenting over the Traces*? Because now that I'm done I realize it has all the themes of an Arabic epic poem: the sorrowful visit to former haunting grounds; the past glory of the tribe; love and the longing for the absent beloved; fighting; the horse; the hunt.

How do you figure that? The hunt?

Dogs and deer in the forest. And the hunt for the rapist. Allow me a little poetic license! But seriously, I have no idea what to call it.

Hmm . . . Why don't you call it Love Is Like Water? *Because love is the common thread. Not always in the sense your grandmother meant; there are so many different kinds of love. There is another way that love is like water: it finds a way around every obstacle; you can try to dam or divert it but it will manage to trickle around the rocks, no longer the gushing stream it once was, perhaps, but it will find a way to keep flowing.*

Glossary

baladi: countrified.
baltagui: bully.
fellaha: peasant (fem.).
fellahin: peasants.
habibti: an endearment.
haram: wife.
hijab: headcovering.
iftar: the meal that breaks the fast at sunset during Ramadan.
Inshallah: God willing.
karimat: daughter.
khawaga: foreigner, westerner.
nadart: I have pledged.
Om: mother of.
pasionaria: Spanish Civil War heroine.
rais: chief, leader, president.
Sitt: lady.
sohour: last meal before beginning the fast at dawn during
    Ramadan.
suffragi: waiter or butler.
yallah: come on.
zaghruta: trill of rejoicing produced by vibrating the tongue.
zawiya: Islamic religious school.